The Silence of the Missing

Rick R. Reed

Spectrum Books

Paperback ISBN: 978-1-915905-16-1

First edition, Spectrum Books, 2023

Discover more LGBTQ+ books at www.spectrum-books.com

Contents

For Bruce, my heart and my inspiration...always.

"The first kiss can be as terrifying as the last."
— *Daina Chaviano, The Island of Eternal Love*

"Before we belonged to anyone else, we were each other's."
— *Elizabeth Noble, The Way We Were*

"The silence of the dead says, Goodbye.
"The silence of the missing says, Find me."
— *Dennis Lehane, Gone, Baby, Gone*

Chapter 1

Now—Sam

The metallic bark of the door buzzer startled me out of reading Stephen King's *Fairy Tale*. And I was just getting to the first good part of what I knew would be many. King had been my literary hero since I was thirteen years old and picked up a movie tie-in paperback of *Carrie* in a used bookstore. I hated being pulled out of his world.

"Shit. What fresh hell is this?" I mumbled. I closed the book reluctantly and stood.

It was a Saturday morning in June, the early summer sun pouring in through the four windows of my condo living room. That damn buzzer! I'd *just* settled in on the couch, Bluetooth speaker streaming a George Winston playlist, a steaming cup of Earl Grey on the end table beside me. Marc was out at the gym. Our rescue dog, Vito, a mix of Boston terrier and pug, snored on the floor at my feet. I couldn't imagine a more contented home scene.

A perfect quiet weekend morning—the kind we introverts adore. God, I'd waited for this. I'd gotten King's book from Amazon at the beginning of the week, but waited until now to settle down and savor it—my blessed and peaceful alone time.

The buzzer sounded again—had it always sounded so

annoying, so intrusive? So impatient?

I sighed and set the book down. "Jesus. No rest for the wicked." Longingly, I gazed at my tea. Vito stirred, lifting his heavy head from the rug, and gave a small grumble and snort. He, too, seemed annoyed with the interruption. He'd never been much of a watchdog and hardly ever barked.

I moved to the front door and pressed the intercom button. *I swear to God if this is a Jehovah's Witness...*

"Yeah?" I immediately regretted my tone and hoped my irritation didn't come through. Whomever was out there didn't deserve it. Besides, it might be Marc, who'd forgotten his keys—yet again.

"Sammy Blake?" A man's voice came through.

I paused, head cocked, finger hovering above the *speak* button. No one had called me Sammy since I was a kid, back in eastern Ohio. I'd thought that part of my past was dead. Life in the foothills of the Appalachians now seemed like days that had happened to someone else. Once I'd grown into a man, I found a different life, a different me. No one knew the person I was back then. Often, I thought, neither did I.

"Who is this?" Maybe it was irrational, but I felt a prickle of nerves at the back of my neck. The fine hairs there stood on end.

There was a pause. Vito sniffed at my calves and pawed at me, whining. To him, my proximity to the front door meant only one thing—we were headed out for a walk. I glanced down at him and shook my head. "No. Not right now. Do you see a leash in my hand?"

"An old friend," came the reply. "Can you buzz me in?"

Okay, this is weird. I wasn't expecting anybody, not

even a delivery. The fact that this person called me by my childhood name was kind of surreal and creepy. In spite of my misgivings, I was curious. Who wouldn't be?

Still, I didn't feel comfortable buzzing him in. This was Chicago, after all, where murder was commonplace and crime was part of the city's identity. Most people, even in so-called *safe* neighborhoods, were careful about who they let into their home. Yet, this person knew my name, so this couldn't be some random weirdo ringing condo building intercoms to get inside. Long ago, the homeowner's association had decided we would *not* put names next to intercom buttons outside, for just this purpose. The unit number, especially in a crime-ridden metropolis like Chicago, was enough.

No. This is a specific weirdo. Who knows your name...

I decided in the moment that what made the most sense was to simply go downstairs and find out who this person was and what he wanted. "Gimme a sec," I said. "I'll be right down."

I was in a robe and a pair of plaid flannel boxers. I hurried into the bedroom and pulled yesterday's jeans and T-shirt off a chair that existed solely for the purpose of collecting cast-off clothing, much to my neatnik husband's chagrin. I dressed quickly and hurried down the stairs to the lobby.

Through the glass front door, I could see him—a man about my age with dark hair, red-rimmed round glasses, and a tall, lanky build. *Ichabod Crane. The Scarecrow.*

No clue.

I patted my pocket, making sure my house keys were there, and headed out to join him in the courtyard.

I smiled, despite my nerves. Seeing him rung absolutely no bells. "Hello. I'm Sam." I cocked my head. "And you are?"

He grinned back. "This is weird."

"Uh, yeah, it certainly is." I narrowed my eyes. "Do I know you?"

He held out his hands, palms up. His expression was neutral, yet I swore I detected a bit of hope in it. The sun caught and lightened the green of his irises and, for just a moment, there was a sense of déjà vu. "You used to."

The day was warm, humid. Bees buzzed. The sun blazed. The air was still.

Yet an icy chill ran down my spine.

"I did? I don't recall. I'm sorry—I'm drawing a blank."

He leaned closer, his gaze boring into my own. I wanted to jump back.

His voice was soft, as though he hoped to confide a secret. "I'm Jeb. Kleber. You remember me, right? Summers on the banks of the Ohio? Boyhood secrets? A love that dare not speak its name?" He raised his eyebrows. A smile made the corners of his eyes crinkle.

My blood turned to ice.

Everything inside dried up, as if all the moisture had been drained out of my system. Dizziness washed over me. I reached out a hand behind me, grasping for something solid, but all that was there was sticky summer air. "No. No, you're not. That's not possible."

He nodded. "It *is* possible. In fact, it's true. I know it's hard to believe."

I shook my head, trying to gather some spit so I could swallow. "Go away. You can't be him. He's gone. Dead." Suddenly, I wanted to turn and run back inside, dash up the stairs, and, once alone, sob for the missing boy I'd once loved.

"*Not* dead. Obviously. Disappeared is the better term." He eyed me, imploring me, I thought, to be reasonable, to see shades of distinction.

People don't disappear for more than thirty years with no explanation. Not commonly, anyway. People who disappear for three decades were most likely dead.

Suddenly, I was swept back. In my mind's eye, I was a thirteen-year-old boy in love for the first time with a fellow white trash boy, living in the foothills of the Appalachians with my single mom.

"Obviously, I'm very much alive." He shook his head, expression mournful. "It's a long story." He looked up at the building, a vintage white-brick courtyard that had been gutted and redone five years ago when Marc and I moved in. "Can you just let me come in, please? I'll only take a few minutes. I can explain."

I shook my head and turned toward the front door. I pulled my keys out. "I don't think that's a good idea."

"Please. Sammy."

I had my key in the lock.

"Wait," he said.

I should have gone in. I should have ignored his one-word request or command and gotten myself back inside. I should have double locked the door behind me. But *should-haves* were the saddest form of regret there was—and I've never been good at them, so I turned back. My hands trembled. I wanted to pinch myself to ensure I was awake. But I knew, deep in my bones, this was no dream.

He wore a pale green and brown Henley and cargo shorts. He reached up and pulled aside the opening of the shirt at his throat. A slender silver chain rested against his smooth skin and on it, a purple amethyst pendant. It caught the sunlight and flashed.

For a moment, the world shimmered and then went dark for just a second, not long enough for me to actually faint, but enough to make me slump against the heavy glass of the vestibule door. I drew in several deep breaths and tried to calm my quaking hands enough to turn the key in the lock and to open the door. I turned back to him.

"You should come in." And I moved toward the darkness of the cooler vestibule, heading toward the stairs, knowing he'd follow.

He always did.

Chapter 2

1986—Sammy

I

"Why on earth do you want to bring *him*, for God's sakes? That boy's nothing but poor white trash." My mom, Trudy Blake, eyed me over the breakfast table on a sun-drenched morning at the start of July. I had a bowl of Apple Jacks in front of me and she had her usual—black coffee and buttered toast. "I thought we talked about how the people you associate with reflect on you, on your choices. You can be better through them." She bit off a piece of toast and chewed. "You're only as good as the company you keep."

I rolled my eyes. "Better *through* them, Mom? Seriously? Through what? Osmosis? Jeb is a good guy. Decent. And if he's poor white trash, then so are we," I said. "I can't believe you, my mom, are saying I should choose friends based on some kind of social status. Jeez." I didn't dare mention that her two best friends, a woman who called herself Mikey and another called Punkin, both had had brushes with the law. Both women were cool, kind, funny, friendly, but neither was known around St.

Clair for their sterling reputations.

"He lives in a trailer." Trudy slid the plastic milk jug across the table.

I doused my cereal with more milk and took a bite. I chewed, swallowed and said, "So what?" I took a glance around our kitchen, with its cracked linoleum floor, faded faux wood paneling, its Harvest gold appliances, and the faucet that never stopped dripping. "This is hardly a palace."

Trudy finished up her toast and shoved her plate away. She took up her coffee, blew on it, and took a sip. "Where did you get that smart mouth?" She was smiling.

"Maybe from dear old dad?"

The smile drooped at the corners, transitioning into an angry frown. "Careful," she warned. "I won't have my smart ass kid throwing my past up at me."

The sad truth was that neither of us knew who my dad was. Trudy had gone through a wild, rebellious phase during her teens, mainly as a reaction to her Evangelical Christian parents. Smoking, drinking, a little experimenting with drugs, and many, many men. She'd wound up kicked out when she became pregnant at sixteen, with no idea who to turn to for any kind of support. But, even as a high school dropout with a baby, she'd managed to keep a roof over our heads, feed her baby boy, and stay afloat (barely) financially. My father was a mystery that would most likely never be solved—unless there was some miracle revolving around 23andMe and a fantastic coincidence.

"Sorry, Mom." I dropped my spoon beside my bowl and lifted it to slurp up the last of the sweet milk. I did it for two reasons—I loved the dredges of super-sugary milk and, two, drinking from the bowl annoyed Mom.

I shouldn't have tried to irritate her. She'd always done the best she could for the two of us. Whenever I bemoaned our sorry-ass house, our piece-of-shit car, and our general lack of prospects, she always told me, "We may not have much, but we have enough." I retraced my conversational steps, knowing that my wise-acre approach wasn't gaining me any points. "Sorry. We got off track here." I hoped I'd shaped my face into the picture of contrition. "Please, could Jeb come with us to the Fourth of July fireworks or not? I'd really like to bring him."

She stood and cleared the table, rinsing the dishes in the sink. Facing the window over the sink, she said, "I have to get myself ready to go in." She worked across the river, at a commercial pottery in West Virginia, where she stood on her feet above a hot plate for eight hours a day, waxing as-yet-unglazed pottery for piece-work pay. She'd been at the job since she was seventeen. It was hard work and she came home exhausted after every shift. She often fell asleep on the living room sofa shortly before six. "You be sure to wash these dishes up before you go outside, okay?"

"Sure thing, Ma. But what about—"

She turned and cut me off. "And of course you can bring your friend. Thank you for asking first." She brushed by me on the way to the bathroom.

I watched her go. Sometimes, we were mistaken for brother and sister, even though I was thirteen and she was just about to turn thirty. But she was small, barely over five feet, and weighing right around a hundred pounds sopping wet. Put her black hair in pigtails and she'd be mistaken for my *younger* sister.

What I didn't say was that Jeb was more than a friend. We'd been proving that on a daily basis down on the banks of the Ohio, groping, experimenting, and exploring since late spring.

What I didn't say was that I was in love.

II

The river sparkled in the sun—diamonds cast upon the mud-brown waters.

Jeb and I had taken the rickety wooden steps down the steep bank to the pebbled shore and now sat on an old plaid blanket he'd brought from home. He'd also snagged a couple of Iron City beers and a bag of Cool Ranch Doritos—his idea of a grown-up picnic. I agreed—and the cold beer, bitter, hoppy, and delightful, made me feel wild and rebellious.

We'd spent the day foraging on the riverbank. We'd often found cool stuff washed up on shore, along with the usual assortment of junk—old tires, small appliances, numerous cans, condoms, once even a full mannequin. That had been a shock, because at first glance I was horrified, thinking we'd stumbled across a corpse.

But the treasures made the foraging fun and worthwhile. There was contorted driftwood that, with a little work and polish on my part, could be transformed into something beautiful. There were examples of my found art all around our little house in the east end of St. Clair. Mom had one on her bedroom dresser and on it, she hung all her necklaces.

One time, we'd found a man's watch. The links appeared to be solid gold, even though the watch itself no longer worked. The back was engraved with "Terry and Butch—HOLLAND." I'd learned that HOLLAND stood for "Hope our love lasts and never dies." I wondered if Terry and Butch were a same-sex couple. Had their "forever" relationship outlived the tragic fate of the lost or cast-off timepiece?

We'd also once found a vaguely dissatisfying stash of porn hidden behind the trunk of a maple tree. The magazines were all *Hustlers* and *Playboys*. And, even though they featured women and we'd already known our interests were in men, there remained an illicit thrill to the cache.

One of the *Hustlers*, my favorite, the one that made it home with me, and the issue I still had hidden between my mattress and box springs, showed a threesome—two men and a woman—acting out a baseball locker room fantasy.

Jeb and I, once we were certain we were truly alone and no prying eyes could see us from the top of the riverbank, had spent more than an hour making out. I'd wanted to go further—I always did, but Jeb said he wasn't ready for anything beyond kissing and touching. He'd told me that even those seemingly innocent displays of affection made him feel guilty, but I was simply "too cute to resist."

One day, though, I was hopeful I'd get Jeb to come around to my way of thinking. And that day, I believed, would be the July Fourth fireworks, when I'd convince Mom to let me bring Jeb home afterward. I'd call it a "sleepover," although I believed very little sleep would be accomplished. Dreams come true, maybe.

Smiling at the thought and the prospect, I jumped up, stripped down to my white briefs and jumped in the fast-moving water. It was as warm as a bath. I dog paddled a little way out, toward Harker's Island, the tiny tree-covered strip of land in the middle of the water.

I didn't fail to heed the internal warning that many boys just like me had drowned making such a journey. The Ohio's fast-moving currents were often hidden and could be treacherous. Actually, I was forbidden to swim in the river or even to play on its banks.

But what kid listened to that advice when the river was so close and offered so much?

I got out a few feet, where I could no longer touch the muddy bottom, and turned over to float on my back. The sun glinted down, hot, and the water buoyed me up like a cork. *This is a little bit of heaven*. I lifted my head to scream, "Get in here!" to Jeb.

It didn't take a lot of convincing.

Before the sun even hit high noon, we were on Harker Island, alone and exploring the lean-to camps boaters had created on its shores for fishing, impromptu barbeques and beer busts. Sometimes, we'd find leftover cans of beer or discarded condoms.

As we rested, panting, on a patch of grass, Jeb turned to me, "You know I really love you."
I thought the sun had nothing on the warmth it emitted when compared to Jeb's simple, yet complex, declaration.

I peered into his green eyes, lit up even more by the July sun. I saw only affection and truth there. "I love you too. And I always will."

After we'd been on the island for an hour or so, clouds moved in to the east—they were dark, foreboding, hanging low on the horizon. The ozone smell of imminent rain arose. We decided we'd better head back. "The last thing we need is to get caught in the middle of the river with lightning striking. Jesus."

We hurried to the river's edge and hoped we'd have time to make it back to shore before the rain started—or the storm took hold.

A flash of heat lightning, white, lit up the dark clouds in the distance. The air grew cooler. Thunder grumbled.

"Wait." I stopped in my tracks. There it was, hanging on the lowest branch of a tree. A silver chain, cheap, with a small piece of violet quartz attached as a pendant. It swung in the breeze that was rapidly becoming a gust. Amethyst. I recognized the quartz stone from the geology portion of science class last year. I was pretty sure amethyst, according to Mr. Pletcher, our science teacher, had protective qualities.

And I wanted, more than anything, to protect Jeb as we made our journey across the river.

He was ahead of me, already knee deep in the water. In a moment, he'd be in up to his waist and would move his arms above his head to dive in, gracefully parting the greenish brown water.

I grabbed the pendant from the branch and hurried toward him. Once I could, I threw the chain over his head, almost like a lasso. It settled around his neck and hung down just below his collarbone. I kissed the back of his neck.

He turned to me in surprise, one hand touching the purple stone. "What's this?"

"I just found it. Hanging there on that tree. Finders keepers, right?" I turned to point and then turned back. "I was meant to give it to you." I grinned. "For protection."

His eyes grew misty, soft, reminding me of the color of moss. "But what will protect you?"

"You, of course. Now let's get going. Those clouds are getting blacker, and I think there's more than just a shower on the way."

We both hurried into the river, whose surface was now rippled by the wind, as gray as the sky above.

Wordlessly, we raced each other back to shore.

III

St. Clair was a town of only ten thousand souls, but you wouldn't know it from their annual fireworks display. Shot off from a barge in the Ohio River, the night sky lit up in brilliant blooms of color for more than twenty minutes every July Fourth. Town roads were filled with potholes. The downtown was a sad conglomeration of boarded-up storefronts for businesses that had thrived, petered out, and died, especially when the steel mill just east of us on the Pennsylvania border closed, back when Mom was a girl. But the town's poverty didn't stop St. Clair from putting on an awesome Independence Day celebration every year. Somehow, they found the funds for an extended, loud, and patriotic display.

Mom and I had our secret spot for viewing. Each year, we were amazed that no one else had discovered it, because the viewpoint had to be the best in town.

Mom had known about it since she was a little girl and her father would take her hiking in the hilly wilderness bordering the town, looking for mushrooms. Off Acton Road, there was a dirt driveway to an abandoned house, which, to be honest, looked like something out of a horror movie. I wouldn't have been surprised to see Leatherface himself, or maybe Michael Myers, emerge from behind its peeling, rusty-hinged front door. Weathered gray wood, falling-down gutters, a weed-infested yard filled with decaying auto parts, and broken-out windows made for a nightmare-inducing setting. The place had been a mystery for decades—complete with rumors that someone had been murdered in the house—and it was probably the reason no one ever ventured up the steep, blackberry-vine-choked hillside behind it.

No one, that is, except my family.

Once we hiked our way up that challenging rise, we were rewarded—big time. At the top of the hill was a path that ran along a steep drop-off in the direction of the river. Looking down from its height, you could see the whole valley open up—the brownish curving snake of the Ohio, Harker Island, barges making slow progress on the muddy water, the houses and small businesses rising along both tree-covered hillsides on the Ohio side and the northern panhandle of West Virginia side. It was glorious and breathtaking, even without the promise of fireworks.

We headed up there now. Mom, Jeb, and I lugged a cooler filled with pop, Mom's egg-salad sandwiches, chips, and my favorite—chocolate cupcakes with maple frosting.

The day was winding down into dusk and the sunlight was a perfect peach-colored hue at the edge of the horizon. Below us, traffic along Route 7 slowed, some of the cars even pulled over on the side of the road to watch the fireworks. A crowd also gathered at the wharf just off of downtown. Some of them were on foot, but many idled in small motor boats. There were even a few jet skis circling in the dark water.

Distant music drifted up to us. I could make out Madonna singing, 'Papa, Don't Preach,' the Pet Shop Boys with 'West End Girls,' and Steve Winwood wanting someone to bring him a higher love.

As we settled, the sky morphed from blue to orange, lavender, and gray.

This is going to be a perfect night. Stars began to wink in the darkening sky. There wasn't a cloud in sight.

Mom opened up the cooler and picnic hamper while Jeb and I spread out the large quilt we'd brought, digging its corners down into the soft, grassy earth at our feet. All the while, our dog, Vanilla, a white terrier mix, danced around us, yapping, tail wagging. I'm sure she was hopeful that some of the food we'd brought would come her way. "Don't you worry," I told her, "We have cookies for you, too."

I met Jeb's gaze once we sat. I'd told him earlier in the day that I wanted to let Mom know about my feelings for him. "She'd get it. She really would. I know her. She's not a judger."

"No, no, and again, no." Jeb made his feelings clear. Even though I assured him that the conversation would go no further than the three of us, he was terrified that *my* outing myself to the one person I loved most in the world (besides Jeb, himself, of course) would somehow jeopardize his own closely guarded public image. Jeb played football at East Junior and, in the summer, baseball. His dad came to all the games. Girls loved him. No one suspected him of being gay. Not like they did bookish, quiet, and movie-musical-adoring me.

I didn't even bother to try to hide it.

I knew Jeb wasn't ready, but that didn't stop me from being impatient. At least he'd agreed to spend the night at our house. I wouldn't force anything, of course, but my fantasies had been in high gear all day.

IV

The fireworks weren't a disappointment.

The display lasted even longer than usual. The grand finale came close to inducing serious hearing loss. All of us loved it, even our weirdo dog, Vanilla, who had never been one of those canines who cower at loud noises like thunder and, well, fireworks. She lay calmly beside me the whole time, occasionally glancing up at the sky, cocking her head. She had a Nylabone to chew on and my comforting hand scratching behind her ears to keep her settled. As long as she was with us, she was happy.

And so was I.

Once the pyrotechnics show was over and the crowds near the river below us dispersed and when the wind washed away the gunpowder scent, we began to gather our things up.

Jeb whispered to me, "Can we hurry? I really gotta pee."

I snorted. "So? Go take a piss." I wiggled my eyebrows at him. "You want me to hold it for you?"

"Shut up." He eyed my mom. "What about her?"

"She's not allowed to hold it for you."

He blew out a big sigh. "You're hopeless, man. Someone should lock you up."

"Go over there." I pointed to a copse of maple and pine trees. "Mom's not going to give a frig if you take a leak out here. What? You think she'd torture you? Make you wait until we drove home? For what? Good manners?"

He trudged away. Trees and shadows swallowed him

up. Watching him vanish into the darkness gave me a little chill, despite the warm night air. I shivered.

As we packed up the cooler and picnic basket, Mom said, "I owe you an apology."

"For what?"

"For the things I said yesterday about Jeb. It wasn't fair. It was beneath him and it was beneath me. He's a nice boy and you're lucky to have him as your friend."

"Thanks, Mom." I eyed the darkness he'd vanished into. I leaned close to her and, without letting my little ineffectual and annoying inner censor interfere, I blurted the truth out. "He's more than a friend." I laughed. "I love him."

She touched my face for a moment. "Oh, honey, I could see *that*. But I needed you to say it first. So thank you for sharing that with me. It's all good, my sweetie."

"He wouldn't want you to know, so, for now, could we keep this just between us? Please."

She made the universal sign for zipping her lips shut. "Not a word. You let me know when you're ready. I wouldn't dream of saying anything, especially if Jeb isn't in a good place to come to grips with the truth." She glanced toward the woods. I turned my head, expected to see him emerge, but there was only the dark and the wind.

I peered closer, worried Jeb would have overheard us. It was paranoid, I know. But I wasn't sure how he'd react. He wouldn't be happy, that's for sure. And believe me, making him happy was top on my agenda for tonight. I could just about see him, in his faded cut-offs and Cleveland Browns T-shirt, coming back while zipping his fly.

But the image was a figment of my imagination.

All of a sudden, it got quiet—even the wind stilled. Vanilla slumbered on the folded up blanket, paws outstretched. The sound of car and boat horns was completely gone. After the moment of silence, the leaves rustled in the trees, sounding sand-papery and ghostly.

How long has it been? Why's it taking him so long?

Mom glanced toward the woodsy area where Jeb had gone to take a leak. "I'd ask if he fell in, but that doesn't apply." She let out a half-hearted chuckle. Despite the snort of laughter, her expression revealed a smidge of worry. It had been too long. But what explanation could there be?

He'd been gone now, I was sure, for fifteen minutes or so. A nagging sense of worry crept up, tickling the base of my spine. *What's taking him so long?*

Mom tapped me on the shoulder. She was now standing. "Go check on him, okay? I have to get home and get to bed. Tomorrow's a workday, you know. I don't get to sleep in until noon like some people."

"Sure." I wandered toward the woods and noticed for the first time how eerie it was. Once under the canopy of trees, it was very still—and utterly dark—pitch black. Like you-can't-see-your-hand-in-front-of-your-face dark.

"Jeb?"

Only the wind answered, and then the hoot of an owl. My skin crawled. I took a few more steps into the darkness. "Jeb? C'mon, man, this isn't funny. My ma wants to get home."

There was nowhere for him to go. This place, really, was nothing more than a cliff at the top of a hillside. The woods around me bordered the valley, but didn't lead to anywhere significant—certainly no place like a road. The only way out was the way we'd come up.

Or that's what I believed, anyway.

Of course, there was another way out, through the horror-movie-scary woods running in the opposite direction, but I didn't find this out until much later.

The alternative was to think that Jeb finally got cold feet about me, about our budding relationship. In a fit of shame or remorse, maybe he used having to pee as an excuse to slip away. I suppose he could have braved the darkness and descended the hillside without using the main in-out route. It made some sense because what lay ahead would be our first night together. The image of his worried face popped into memory when I told him we'd have to share my full-size bed, with what was probably a leer.

Yet I couldn't believe he'd be so cruel as to just leave me here, worrying not only me, but my mom. Jeb was a lot of things, but one of them was *not* a prankster. Nor was he the kind of person to just ditch other people without an explanation. No, he was kind to a fault and hiding like this, scaring us, wouldn't occur to him. I knew that much for sure. It wasn't in the makeup of the boy I thought I knew so well.

After too many minutes of standing helpless in the pitch darkness and after too long listening to the wind and hoping for a voice or a footfall, I gave up.

He wasn't here.

My eyes had adjusted to the dark and, other than the far-off scurrying of some animal in the underbrush and the occasional hoot of an owl, it was silent. I'd gone in fairly deep and there was no one human here, I thought, other than myself.

I called out for him one more time, hoping against hope he'd answer, but my rational mind taunted me. I knew, with deep-down certainty, he was no longer here. The thought made me sick to my stomach. *Where could he have gone?*

I emerged out of the woods to find Mom waiting, holding Vanilla in her arms like a baby. She cocked her head, her eyebrows coming together in confusion when she saw I was alone. "Sammy? What's going on? Is he okay?"

It took me a moment to find my voice. "He's not there."

"Wait. What? I don't get it." She took a few steps toward the entrance to the woods.

"Mom. I said he isn't there."

"He's gotta be. Where could he go?" She handed me Vanilla, sighing with impatience. "You stay here." She marched off into the woods with a determination that screamed *Let Mom take care of things*. Because, obviously, her boy wasn't capable.

For once, I hoped she was right.

I listened as she made her way into the woods, the crunching of leaves underfoot, a small gasp when she must have run headlong into a tree trunk.

She emerged ten minutes or so later, her face a mask of worry and confusion. There were scratches on her forehead. There wasn't much power behind her voice as she said, "You're right. He's not there. No one is."

I felt a lump the size of a tangerine in my throat, the stinging burn of tears in my eyes. "What could have happened? Where could he be?"

Mom shook her head. "I don't know, honey. I don't know. I wish I did." She stared off for a moment into the shadows. Then she looked at me. "We need to get home."

"We can't just leave without him."

"Sweetie, you looked. *I* searched. We both know he isn't there." She glanced down at her watch. "It's been, like, a half hour, maybe more, since he wandered off."

"Maybe he's lost?"

"Oh Sammy, I don't think so. He said he was going to use the bathroom. Why wouldn't he just do that and come back?"

I had no answer.

She took a step closer. "We need to get home so we can call his family and the cops." She shook her head and my own fear and terror were reflected in her own eyes. "There's probably going to be a rational explanation. We'll laugh about this tomorrow."

I didn't think so. In fact, I wondered, in that moment, with the smell of fireworks still lingering in the close night air, if I'd ever laugh again.

V

We didn't laugh about his disappearance the next day, nor the next, nor the one after that.

We never laughed, because Jeb never came back.

Over the course of July, the whole town united to do everything they could to find him. Our small local police force went above and beyond in their search, organizing volunteer groups to literally beat the bushes in the fields and woods surrounding our small town. Grids were set up; search dogs were deployed. Divers came in from Pittsburgh and dragged the Ohio and a couple of nearby lakes. A tip line was established. Flyers plastered the town—shop windows, telephone poles, and on any surface that could be used as a bulletin board.

For a while, it was all anyone talked about—how the Kleber boy vanished into thin air just after the bursting lights and booms of a Fourth of July fireworks display.

Jeb's parents, distraught, went on three local network news stations to make tearful, impassioned pleas for the return of their son. I watched them on the little portable Mom kept on the kitchen counter, so she could view her soaps while she washed dishes or made supper. Jeb's mom looked tired—dark bags under her eyes, her platinum-dyed hair greasy and plastered to her head. Her eyes shone with tears ready to fall. His dad was a scarecrow—emaciated in a faded red and black plaid flannel shirt too warm for summer—with about as much emotion. His eyes were dark and dead.

Callers deluged the tip lines in the early days with

sightings.

Jeb was with an older man with a shaved head in a black Lincoln Continental.

Someone spotted him at the Orange Julius in the Beaver Valley Mall.

He was with a gang of young, presumably runaway, teenage boys in a bad neighborhood in Akron.

And then something happened that made us all catch our breaths at the end of August. A body was discovered by a couple of boys fishing on the banks of the Ohio. His corpse was tangled up in branches overhanging the churning waters. About the same height and weight as Jeb, folks around town, especially me, Mom, and Jeb's parents were horrified, certain that Jeb had been found.

But no.

The body turned out to be that of Bill Humphrey, an unemployed welder. He'd been in debt. His wife had left him, taking their two kids, a boy, seven and a girl, twelve. Folks around town who'd seen the man in recent weeks gossiped about how they hadn't seen him sober in a long time. Most likely in an alcoholic haze, he'd waded into the river one night, hopeless and not wanting to face another morning.

The death was ruled accidental, but we'd all believed it was suicide.

A new school year started and with it, my entry into high school as a freshman. The phrase "vanished into thin air" become one I couldn't bear to hear. I had trouble concentrating. My grades slipped. I just didn't seem to have an interest in anything.

Mom didn't bring me up to be religious. She wasn't a spiritual person, and she raised me to think the bible and its accounts were nothing more than that—stories, fairy tales. There was no bearded man in the sky, picking and choosing who he would and wouldn't look out for, according to her. "All we have is right here on earth," she'd say. "Heaven and hell are with us in the here and now and the funny thing is, one day what was heaven can be hell—and vice versa."

From as far back as I can recall, her atheism made sense. In our tiny, rundown rental house, with its eccentric water and unpredictable heat in the winter, it was easy to imagine there was no great protector in the sky.

But this lack of belief didn't stop me from praying every night for months. I'd get on my knees next to my bed, clasp my hands together, bow my head, and then beseech a being I couldn't even imagine returning to my first love. Or, if this deity was unable to fulfill my selfish wish, then could he at least make sure Jeb was okay, wherever he was.

I never got an answer.

Not from god or anyone else.

As the school year went on and on, into Christmas break, Jeb's disappearance got less and less notice. Other news stories took precedence. Conversations about Jeb were less frequent and finally, they, like him, vanished. He would never be found, I worried, neither dead nor alive. There were no phone calls. The sightings reported on the tip line fell off and then died altogether. The line was closed.

People were done looking.

Jeb was yet another face on a milk carton. A mystery that most likely would never be solved.

Forgotten.

That Christmas, my mom asked me to take a tin of her pizzelle cookies over to the Klebers. She knew their holidays would be anything but festive and wanted to make some small gesture to let them know we were thinking of them in this horrible time, when the whole world seemed to have left them behind as they celebrated.

I'd tried to stop by frequently after Jeb went missing, but no one ever answered the door. I'd come prepared to cut their little square of grass in front of the trailer and later, ready to rake leaves, and even later, shovel snow. These acts of kindness, I figured, were for deserving people. Besides, they'd make me, in a strange way, feel closer to Jeb. But I never got the chance.

Cookies in hand, I didn't have much hope anyone would answer, but I got a surprise this time.

Mrs. Kleber, Mandy to everyone in town, opened the door a crack to peer out at me. The day was heavy with the scent of imminent snow and dark charcoal clouds pressed close to the hills on the horizon.

"Oh hi, Sammy. What's up, hon?"

She wore a frazzled expression. Her dark roots now traveled down to just about the tips of her ears. She had on an old, faded green sweatshirt, frayed at the bottom, moth-eaten, and a pair of men's flannel sleep pants. Her skin was sallow and her irises floated in pale red.

I held up the cookie tin. "Mom sent these. They're pizzelles, Italian Christmas cookies. They're really good." I smiled.

She looked down at the red and green tin as though I was offering a plate of excrement. She opened her mouth, closed it again, and then stared at me.

I held the tin closer to her. "Go on. Please take

it." I remembered another woman, a cheerful, brassy, loud-mouthed mother who laughed a lot, told dirty jokes, and made fun of everyone. No one was beneath her contempt and she never failed to crack me up.

Until today.

She reached out a hand that looked as though it might belong to a ninety-year-old—veiny, the parchment skin hanging on for dear, withered life. She took the cookie tin and set it down somewhere in the shadows behind her.

"Thank you, and please tell your mom the same." She moved to close the thin aluminum door. When I didn't turn away, she asked, "Is there something else?"

I stared and debated whether I should just leave her alone in her grief and misery. All appearances indicated that was what she wanted, heartless as it might feel on my part.

But I couldn't simply leave it at that. I cocked my head, met her worn-out gaze and asked, "Are you okay?"

She sighed and for a moment consulted the dark clouds. "What do you think, boy?"

The chill I felt was not coming from the wind whipping up out of the north. I felt heat rise to my cheeks. "Stupid question."

"Yeah, very stupid." She stepped back and opened the door wider. "You wanna come in for a minute? Place is a mess, but...whatever."

I stepped around her to go inside the dark trailer. She wasn't kidding about the mess. First, the place reeked of stale smoke. Every surface was covered with cast-off clothing that looked as though it wouldn't even pass muster as a Goodwill donation. The surfaces of the end tables and coffee tables in the living room were hidden under grease-stained pizza boxes, dirty paper plates, beer cans, and overflowing ashtrays.

I almost missed Jeb's dad on the couch, turned toward the back and snoring.

When I turned to Mandy, she was watching me. "Jealous of our happy home?"

"Oh Mandy, I'm so sorry."

She nodded and her eyes were shiny with tears. Had no one come to offer comfort? Cookies? Support?

This seemed like hell, a place where joy and hope went to die.

Their trailer had always been a mess, but before it was organized chaos. There was always music, usually heavy-metal that set my teeth on edge, but I could always count on chatter and laughter to compete with the soundtrack.

"You don't have to stay." She put a head to her forehead, as though an icepick were stabbing her behind her eyes. "I really wish you wouldn't, actually. I don't know what I was thinking." The last sentence she murmured to herself, not looking at me.

I got it. I wasn't offended. I held out a hand to touch her shoulder, and she stumbled back and out of reach.

"Please go."

"Merry Christmas." I turned to the door, regretting the words immediately.

But the only answer I got was silence.

As I opened the door, she said, "I know."

I turned. "Know what?"

"What you were to Jeb. And what he was to you. You must miss him." Tears stood out on her cheeks as she hunted around for a pack of cigarettes on the counter.

There was so much I wanted to say, but once she found her smokes and lit one, she looked at me like I was one more cockroach in the place. "Are you still here?" she wondered through a cloud of blue-gray smoke.

I hurried out, heartbroken.

The school year concluded and the humid days of another summer approached. I despaired because one day I realized I was having trouble remembering Jeb's face or the sound of his voice.

Life's cruel lesson became clear to me as I celebrated my fourteenth birthday. Nothing—and no one—lasts forever.

Or so I thought.

Chapter 3

Now—Sam

I

I stood across from him near the front door.

This is a dream.

This is not a dream.

We were simultaneously two grown men at the tail-end of our forties and two teenage boys discovering our sexuality for the first time and realizing how love and lust intertwine and can be all-consuming.

I didn't know what to say. I wrung my hands, noticing how damp they were. I wasn't certain where to rest my gaze. *Could this really be Jeb?* After all these years, it was hard, maybe even impossible, to say. This man had the same green eyes, the same lanky build and dark straight hair—even all grown up. And the pendant! A flash of memory revealed a vision of me affixing it to his damp neck in the river. I could even recall the kiss I planted on the nape of his neck.

A summer thunderstorm had born down on us. We'd worried about making the passage from Harker's Island to the shore without getting struck or pulled under by the powerful currents we'd been warned against.

I wanted to protect him.

And how did this person know my name? How did he know where to find me? Was he really who he said he was? And if not, how did he know about Jeb?

Once the furor around his disappearance died down, Jeb had faded into tragic obscurity. He was never national news, just one of the thousands of kids who go missing every year.

The questions could drive me insane. His presence, close enough to touch, could drive me insane. And here I was, on a quiet morning in my boring home, wanting nothing more than to sip a cup of tea and read my newest Stephen King book.

The apple cart was truly upset.

I worried that Marc would be home soon. He'd wonder who this stranger standing in our living room was. Jeb's disappearance, back in the summer of '86, was a subject I didn't think I'd ever broached with him. The mystery loomed large through the rest of my teens, of course, but once I'd gone away to Ohio State, gotten my degree and moved to Chicago, I had to admit, my thoughts of Jeb and what had happened that summer at last faded, only revived when I faced a reminder, like Fourth of July fireworks or the curve of a slow-moving river. Or the disappearance of yet another innocent soul...

"Could we sit down?" Jeb interrupted my thoughts. "I just want to talk. I won't take too much of your time."

"Sorry. You have to understand—I'm a little frazzled."

"Of course." He smiled and edged a bit closer.

"Come on." I led him more into the condo. He took

a seat on the couch. I sat opposite, eyeing him. *What do I do in a situation like this? Do I start a pot of coffee brewing? Do I breakout the blueberry scones in the pantry?* The thoughts made me laugh.

"What's funny?"

"Nothing. Nothing at all. That was hysteria," I replied honestly. "Who *are* you? What are you doing here? Forgive me if I'm having trouble believing who you say you are. It just doesn't seem possible."

His eyes took on a faraway cast—he was thinking. He didn't speak for a long time. Making up a story? What could his angle possibly be? Marc and I were doing okay, but we were far from rich, so financial gain was out.

He repeated the stuff he'd said outside, as though if he said it enough, it would ring true in my ears. "I told you who I am—Jeb. Jeb Kleber. We knew each other as boys back in St. Clair, Ohio. Your mom was named Trudy. You lived in a little green-shingled house in the east end of town. You had a little dog, white, fluffy." He cocked his head and squinched his eyes together. "Its name was, um—" He snapped his fingers and smiled. "Vanilla!"

I covered my face with my hands. This was way too much to absorb. How could he possibly know all this stuff? And even more concerning—if he really *was* Jeb, why was he surfacing *now*? Why hadn't he gotten in touch long before?

My gut churned. "So where have you been all these years? What happened that night? You literally vanished into thin air." I leaned forward. "Answer me those questions and maybe I can begin to believe you're really Jeb."

"Have you heard the phrase, 'truth is stranger than fiction?'"

"Who hasn't?"

"You might have trouble believing me and I wouldn't blame you. For one, I did come back to St. Clair, many years ago. Like a lot of folks in our hometown, my dad had ended up with cancer—lung—and my mom was a wreck when he passed away, after a long and painful decline. I don't know that she ever got over him being gone. Far as I could tell, she didn't even want to see me. She was good with me being dead, if not buried."

He swallowed, and I was aware he was holding emotion back. "I guess I forgive her. She'd made peace with my death so long ago that it was too much of a shock, having me back. She couldn't seem to quite get herself to a place where my return was normal, let alone joyful. I think it was just too much."

I could understand, although I didn't voice my feelings aloud.

"How long ago was that?"

"Fifteen years ago or so?" He glanced down at the cracked cement at our feet. "I guess I understood—me being back was too much of a shock, especially after dad's death so close to my return."

His answers weren't setting my mind at ease. No, they were actually causing more confusion, more cognitive dissonance.

I rose and moved to the window overlooking our street, Wolcott. Down below, things were relatively quiet for an urban neighborhood. I always loved our view—on the corner was a large Victorian turn of the century house with a big wraparound porch. Other turn-of-the century apartment buildings, now condos, stood north and south on our block and several adjoining ones. The trees lining our street were mature, ancient, most of them maples. It would be almost bucolic if it weren't for the cars crowding both sides, bumper to bumper. When it was nearly impossible to find a parking place in a neighborhood, bucolic flew out the window.

That was Chicago for you.

Down the street a ways, I spied our little silver Prius pulling into a coveted spot. I murmured, "My husband's home." I watched as it tapped bumpers with the car in front of it and behind it, which was the giveaway that my husband Marc had gotten back from the gym. How would I explain this man in our house? Would Marc think he'd caught me at something? The thought was laughable. We were well past jealousy. We'd done the whole checking each other's phones and internet histories, and unfounded suspicions early in our relationship. After more than a decade together, we'd finally learned to trust and have faith in each other.

Marc got out of the car and leaned across the seat to grab the blue and gray backpack he used as a gym bag. I didn't turn away as he made his way up the street, so much about him familiar—the slight limp from a skateboarding accident when he was a teenager, the dark, wavy hair now salted, the reflection of the sun on the lenses of his tortoiseshell-framed round glasses. He looked fit and trim in his jeans and tank top, a man much younger than fifty-three. At least in my eyes...

I felt more than heard Jeb leave. There was a disturbance in the air behind me, almost as though a draft had managed its way inside, despite our windows being shut against the heat.

When the back door of the kitchen squeaked open

and then closed, I turned.

Jeb was gone.

I wondered for a moment if he had ever really been here. But he had—whoever he was, whatever intent he had.

I'd been about to ask him what he was doing in those years when I'd believed he was missing, if not dead. Why hadn't he gotten in touch with me before? Why had my mom not mentioned his return? It was hard to believe she didn't know about it—in St. Clair, everyone knew everyone else's business. Even though more than a decade had passed—if he'd returned when he claimed—it would have been big news, spreading like proverbial wildfire. Trudy would have been on the phone to me the minute she got wind of it.

The front door opened, and I turned as Marc entered.

He read the look on my face like a page in a book. "What's the matter?"

"I'd tell you, but I'm not sure you'd believe me."

He cocked his head. "What?" He came more fully into the open living area and set his backpack down on the floor. He brushed a hand through his hair.

I gave him a peck on the lips. "Have a seat? You want some iced tea?"

He sat. "Okay, with lemon, if we've got it."

I moved to the refrigerator and pulled out the pitcher. As I was pouring tea, I prepared to spill some different tea. "I have something to tell you," I said without looking at him. "Suspend your disbelief."

II

"And this happened when you were, what, thirteen?" Marc lowered his glasses to peer out at me over the top of the frames with concerned brown eyes.

I nodded. Next to him on the couch, but not looking at him, I'd poured out the whole story of my first love and his odd disappearance on Independence Day, 1986. Stranger, I let him know that a man claiming to be Jeb Kleber had just been in our home fewer than twenty minutes ago. And then, at last, I met his gaze, fearful of what his reaction would be.

"This is crazy," Marc said. "This is like some Lifetime movie kind of shit, ripped from the headlines, as they say." He grinned, but there was little mirth in his expression.

"Tell me about it."

We sat in silence for a few moments. We sipped our iced tea, looking out at the trees, the leaves whispering in the soft breeze. It was bright and sunny, a perfect summer day when we should have been east, at our neighborhood beach, which was walking distance from our condo. It was a time filled with birdsong, human chatter and laughter, music escaping from car windows, the hum of bees.

All of these normal things served to make what had just occurred even more surreal.

And then Marc asked, "What are you gonna do about it? Call the police?"

I shrugged and shook my head. "I don't know. Certainly not call the cops, for god's sakes. He didn't do anything wrong, other than turn my world upside down. I don't like that, naturally, but I hardly think it's a crime." In my mind's eye, I pictured him standing in this very room and again, questioned reality, questioned my own sanity. Had he *really* been here? Or had something subconscious triggered some kind of psychotic break, causing me to hallucinate?

Honestly, I wished I could believe I'd imagined him. After all, there was no trace of him in our place now. But I'd never been one for fantasy. As far back as I could remember, I couldn't recall a single instance where I'd had trouble distinguishing reality from, er, something else. For better or worse, I was grounded in this world and the truth revealed by my own eyes, ear, nose, mouth, and fingers.

No, Jeb had been here. Or at least someone calling himself Jeb had. There was no doubt in my mind.

But what did he want? Why had he resurfaced after all this time? And why did he rush out without a word when I mentioned Marc was home? Why wouldn't he simply stay?

These red flags made me more and more uneasy and yes, a little terrified, the more I pondered them.

Marc scooted closer and put his arm around me. "So weird. But it'll be okay, right? He won't come back, whoever he is, and if he does, he'll have me to deal with."

I wanted to laugh. My husband was a lot of things, but imposing or threatening wasn't on the list of his sterling qualities. But I didn't permit myself to laugh. For one, I didn't want to embarrass him—I was touched by his protectiveness, no matter how ineffectual it might be.

Just the fact that he wanted to look out for me helped allay my fears and made me feel cared for and safe. And for another, there was a nagging sense of hysteria, deep down, telling me that if I dared laugh, I wouldn't be able to stop.

"I wish I could be sure he won't come back." I wasn't certain of that at all.

I wanted to know more.

My mind raced with possibilities. *Had* Jeb been abducted and raised by some weirdo? I could vaguely recall seeing a TV special, maybe on *20/20*, about just such a case—had it happened in California? I tried to come up with a name and drew a blank. But I recalled how a young boy had been abducted and had lived, for years, with a pedophile as his son. And he'd somehow managed to escape when he was a teen.

I'd be googling later, for sure.

But for now, I needed to reassure Marc that this odd appearance posed no threat to us, whether that possibility had crossed his mind or not.

It had crossed mine.

First love is a powerful thing.

III

After dinner, with Marc settled in front of the TV and a Netflix documentary about Jeffrey Dahmer (we were both addicted to true crime stories), I began my Google search. I was settled on the bed, legs stretched out before me, laptop in place. I typed in *boy abducted and found years later*. There was a hope, flickering like a flame in the back of my mind, that the name Jebediah Kleber would surface among the hits. I first went through several pages of the more than thirteen million results, hoping against hope he'd appear. Perhaps I had simply missed the story of how he'd found his way back. It was certainly possible.

But no such name surfaced.

Others did. There was eleven-year-old Shawn Hornbeck, who'd been abducted while riding his bike in a small town outside St. Louis by Michael Devlin. A psychic had proclaimed the boy was dead on national TV, yet he was very much alive. Devlin held him captive for more than four years, when the boy apparently grew too old for Devlin's taste and he abducted another boy—thirteen-year-old Ben Ownby—at a bus stop. Both abductions took place in broad daylight, but the second time, Devlin wasn't as fortunate. Witnesses saw him take Ownby and heard his cries. Their reports led to both boys being found, and the case was dubbed the "Missouri Miracle."

There were other cases of long-term abductions and miraculous returns—Paislee Shultis, Jayme Closs, the very famous case of Elizabeth Smart, Kamiyah Mobley (who was taken as an infant, only to resurface when she was eighteen years old). Jaycee Dugard had been taken at age eleven and kept for eighteen years. There was the case of three young women abducted in Cleveland, Ohio. Michelle Knight, Amanda Berry, and Gina DeJesus were kept prisoner in their captor, Ariel Castro's, home for a decade before being rescued.

The case that resonated most with me, though, was that of Steven Stayner, who'd been taken at age seven in Merced, California and kept for seven years by his abductor, Kenneth Parnell. Despite molestation, Parnell tried to make the boy his son. Stayner attended school and lived openly with Parnell just thirty-eight miles away from his hometown. Who knew how long he would have been kept, had not Parnell abducted five-year-old Timothy White. The presence of the little boy and knowing what he would face, spurred Stayner to rescue him. In a dramatic escape, Stayner (known as Dennis Gregory Parnell) was able to save the five-year-old, becoming a national hero when he returned to his hometown and family. Tragically, Stayner was killed in a motorcycle accident a few years later at age twenty-four.

The Stayner family wasn't done with tragedy, though. Perhaps marked by the trauma of his brother's abduction, Cary Stayner later became a convicted serial killer.

Reading about all these cases validated my concern that not all kids who were taken didn't show up later dead. These cases were the tip of the iceberg.

It was quite possible that Jeb had been taken that night in 1986 and kept by some sicko who wanted a son and/or a sexual slave. I shuddered at the prospect.

The realization also produced another flood of questions.

If Jeb had been abducted on that Fourth of July, how had his abductor known he'd be at our riverside and hilltop lookout? Who'd informed him? Had he been lying in wait in the woods just a few feet away from us? I imagined a dark stranger danger figure lurking in the woods, watching us as we ate our picnic and *ooh-ed* and *ah-ed* over the fireworks display, waiting, waiting, for his moment to pounce on his prey. The image in my head made me tremble.

And if Jeb, like Shawn Hornbeck and Steven Stayner, had been kept for years on end, why hadn't his return garnered more publicity? I remembered, years ago, watching a dramatization of the Stayner case on television. It was called *I Know My First Name is Steven*. Both Stayner and Hornbeck had made national headlines and were the subject of podcasts, books, and cinematic dramatizations. It was simply incredible, in the truest sense of the world, that Jeb had returned some fifteen years ago—as he'd mentioned—and there was not even a ripple in the media about it. Yes, St. Clair was a tiny town in the poor foothills of the Appalachians, but this would be a big human-interest story, regardless. There'd be some trace of it online, right?

Where was the reporting about Jeb's return? Where was *his* true-crime book? Where was *his* miniseries?

I shut the laptop and closed my eyes. There were simply too many red flags. How could I believe this guy who'd shown up out of the mysterious, proverbial blue? And, no matter if his story was true or not, what did he want with me now, after all these years? Was it because we'd once been in puppy love? This would be the strangest meet-cute in the history of romance.

It was all too confounding.

I lay down, curling up into a fetal position, and hoped this person, whoever he was, would never darken my doorstep again.

IV

We are there, on the pebbled banks of the Ohio River. Jeb faces me, knee deep in the mud brown water. He's wearing nothing but the amethyst pendant, and he's fully erect. Yet, seeing what I'd never seen in real life awakened no lust, as it should have. No, there's a sense of terror, of dread.

I move to him in the water.

He takes me in his arms and pulls me close. The muscles in his chest are hard against my own. His penis feels like a snake against my damp denim cutoffs.

He squeezes tighter, tighter.

I lose my breath. Yet, he doesn't stop.

I push against him, trying to scream, but there's no air.

The sky darkens. Thunder rumbles, followed not by flashes of lightning, but bursts of illumination in red, green, and blue—fireworks in the threatening sky.

He pushes me down, down, until all I can see is mucky, silty water.

I gasp and struggle. Bubbles rise to the surface. I continue to hear the boom of distant pyrotechnics, but Jeb doesn't loosen his grip, his fingers now entwined in my hair.

The world dims and then darkens.

V

I woke suddenly, a muffled scream dying on my lips. I lay on the bed for a long time, glad that Marc didn't hear me cry out. There was a light sheen of sweat on my forehead and the terror from the dream clung to me.

I rolled over and grabbed my phone off the nightstand. Even though I was a grown man in my late forties, Mom had always been my first call whenever I was upset, or even its polar opposite, overjoyed. She listened better than anyone I knew, even Marc.

She answered on the second ring.

"Mom? What are you doing?"

"Just got out of the bathtub, so good timing. How's things, Sammy?"

We chatted for a moment about the weather here, the weather there, how she's planning on making vegetable soup for dinner, the leak in her roof, the pain in her lower back. I needed this time to ease into my question, probably because I wasn't sure I wanted to know the answer.

But after a lot of the usual blather that meant little other than a mother-son connection, I came to the reason for my call.

I took a deep breath and dove in. "I had a visitor today. Someone who said he was from St. Clair."

"Oh? Who's that?" Her voice betrayed no suspicion. She was probably thinking an old classmate or neighbor had shown up, wanting a reunion. I was sure Jeb was the furthest thing from her mind. His name hadn't come up in conversation in years, decades maybe. I was sure she'd recall him, but not certain at all she ever thought of him.

I didn't know how to say it, so I just blurted it out. "Jeb Kleber."

There was a long silence on the other end. And then she sort of laughed, but there was no mirth in it, only confusion. "What? What do you mean?"

I relayed how I was simply reading when an unexpected visitor showed up and how he claimed to be Jeb. "It was unreal, in the truest sense of the word."

"Oh sweetheart, that just can't be. Didn't they rule him dead?" She paused again and I could almost hear the wheels turning. "Yeah, they even had a memorial years ago, erected a headstone and everything. There was something like a GoFundMe to pay for it all. I even contributed a few bucks. But gee, that was ages ago."

"I know, Mom." And I did. I'd forgotten about the memorial because it had to have taken place more than twenty years ago. But she reminded me. "But he was *here* and told me his name. He even called me Sammy without any prompting. No one calls me that these days, except for you. I'm just Sam, or sometimes Samuel, if I'm at work...and in trouble." I chuckled, but it didn't dissipate the dread in my gut.

"Well, this is someone playing a joke. Although I have to tell you, that's one sick prank."

"How would anyone know about the whole thing, Mom? I mean, yeah, it was news back in the day, but it wasn't big news like Elizabeth Smart." I used the only missing person I was sure would register on her radar.

"Everything is on record, hon. Even if it's just on microfiche in a library, if people look hard enough, they can find the news stories about Jeb from back then."

I conceded she had a point. But even if someone did do research—and that would be one hell of a deep dive—the big question was what was the motivation. I asked her, "Why, though? What reason could he have for showing up here today?"

"Did he say?"

"No." And I told her how he vanished from the condo as soon as Marc came home, darting out the back door.

"This is creepy," she said. "I don't like it."

"Tell me about it."

"What are you gonna do?"

"I don't know. It doesn't seem like enough to report it to the authorities. But I wanted to ask you. He said something about returning to St. Clair fifteen years ago. He said his dad had passed from lung cancer. And that his mom couldn't bear to see him."

"Not true. Those are lies. The Klebers both died in a fire when their trailer went up. A lot of folks think they were cooking meth, but I don't know. Probably falling asleep with a cigarette is more likely. But, god, when was this?" She paused. "I'm sure it was about eighteen years ago. I remember because I was dating Charles back then. Remember him? Dark beard? Hare lip scar?"

"Vaguely." Mom had only recently given up on dating losers, given up on love, really, only in the past five years or so. Her parade of unsuitable loves just became too much to bear and after much, much trial and error, she'd realized she was better off alone.

"Yeah, yeah. I can probably look it up for you—the stuff about the fire. Everything's online nowadays."

"Yeah, would you? And could you text me a link if you find something?"

She said she would. But I knew she was right. "The fact that he made up a story about his mom and dad really tells that he's not on the up and up. If he's lying about his parents, then he could be lying about who he is."

"Sure, that's it."

"But I don't know how he knew certain things."

"Like what?"

"Like he remembered Vanilla, even her name."

"That is weird. That wouldn't have been in any news stories. It didn't matter." She stopped, thinking. "Maybe he knows somebody from here? Maybe it *is* somebody from here? Did you ever think of that? That would make sense, wouldn't it?"

I'd considered that, of course. "But then, where did he get the amethyst pendant? I gave it to him right before he got snatched. Remember?"

"I don't think I do. Sorry."

Was I losing my memory as well as my mind? I needed to get off this call. I wanted my Marc's comforting arms and words to surround me, to make me oblivious.

"I gotta go. I need to get supper started." But before I said my final goodbye, I said, "One last thing, Mom. And just covering the bases because I believe I already know the answer. But did they ever find a body?"

"Jeb's? No, not that I know of."

Then it could have been him.

"Thanks for the information. I'll let you go. We're still planning on coming home for Thanksgiving."

"I can't wait. Okay, Sammy. I'm glad you called. Try not to worry too much. I know how you are."

"Yeah, I'll try." *Good luck with that.* "If you think of anything else about Jeb or the Klebers, or anyone who might have known them, let me know. It's got to be someone from out there, it's gotta be. But *why*?" I asked the question again, a petulant whine.

"Who knows? This world gets weirder every day. You be careful now, okay? Don't answer the door and, if this guy shows up again, pretend you're not home. Do *not* let him in."

"I won't."

I wish I would have stuck to my promise.

We hung up.

Chapter 4
1986—Trudy

I

Her best friend, Punkin, was endlessly telling Trudy she should get out more. "Girl, you're still young! But you wouldn't know it to look at you, holed up every night in that cracker box with your boy, Sammy. Let me tell you, there's no TV show that can compete with being in the arms of a good man."

And now Trudy wished Punkin could see her—on her first real date in more than three years, ever since that bastard Mike O'Hara dumped her on Christmas Eve. She'd never guessed he was married. But that was a whole 'nother story.

Tonight, Trudy was with a real gentleman. Chris Sgro was soft-spoken, polite, and attractive in a kind of nerdy, bookish way with neatly trimmed, parted-at-the-side sandy brown hair and deep brown eyes behind silver-framed glasses. Most of the guys who hit on Trudy down at The Green Mill wore old jeans, Steelers or Browns T-shirts and hoodies, steel-toed work boots, and either kept their hair long (sometimes in mullets) or military-short. They didn't deviate much for dates, either. Dressing up meant pulling on a clean pair of jeans and sniffing the armpits of a shirt to see if it passed muster for wearing once again.

Chris was different. He dressed up for their date in a pair of pressed khakis, blue button-down shirt, sweater vest, and penny loafers. Punkin would have laughed him out of the Green Mill. Trudy could almost hear her cackling, "What a dweeb!" she'd say.

Trudy appreciated the effort Chris had gone to, not only with his clothes, but with his hygiene. Although he didn't wear cologne, he smelled of Irish Spring and maybe a hint of eucalyptus from his shaving cream. He even sported a little gel in his hair, but only enough to make it shine.

She'd met him just last week at the A&P downtown when she was grocery shopping. Looking back, she saw how corny his approach was—but it was also kind of sweet.

"Do you know how to tell if a melon is ripe?" He held a honeydew out to her, looking helpless, but charming. She immediately liked his smile and wasn't sure, in the moment, if this was a come-on. If it was, she didn't mind.

She took the melon from his hands and looked it over. "It's not about the sniffing, which is what a lot of people think. Look at the color." She turned it a little. "See how this one is creamier yellow rather than some of those?" She pointed to the very green melons in the bin. "That's a good sign. The other thing you want to do is press on the bottom a little bit. There should be some give. Not like your finger will break through, but it shouldn't be rock hard." She handed him back the melon, and he thanked her.

She'd thought he was cute and wondered why she'd never seen him before. St. Clair was small. When she shopped for groceries, she not only was on a first-name basis with most of her fellow shoppers, but also with the cashiers, deli workers, produce folks, and butchers.

She ran into him again in the parking lot. He'd repeated his gratitude for her help—and now Trudy knew for sure he *was* putting the moves on her—and they'd chatted a bit as they stood by her beat-up brown Chevette and his VW van. They talked about the van, how it reminded her of one her dad had had when she was a little girl. She asked him what brought him to town.

"What makes you think I'm not a local?"

Trudy had laughed. "The truth? I know just about everyone in this burg. Lived here all my life. And I'd remember if I'd seen you around. You look like you should be teaching at the high school."

"You know the Sgros?"

The name was an odd one and Trudy had never heard it. She shook her head.

"That's my mom and dad. They moved here five years ago because they wanted to get out of their neighborhood in Youngstown, which was getting really bad. Lots of crime. They live down in Little England?" He cocked his head.

"Oh! Yeah, that's not far from me." Trudy knew the neighborhood well because it was even poorer than her own. It sat just below the river a bit and habitually got flooded. The homes were all run-down wooden affairs, little more than shacks, often covered with tar paper masquerading as brick.

He nodded and glanced at his watch. "Unfortunately, Ma's sick. Breast cancer. Dad just brought her home from the nursing home in Wheeling." He stared down at the ground for a moment. "There wasn't any more they could do. She isn't expected to last long."

Trudy put her hand on his arm. "I'm so sorry."

"It's okay. I'm just glad I could get time off work to be with her."

Trudy nodded and was about to get in her car. The ice cream in one of the bags would not take kindly to the heat and she couldn't afford to waste food, even food that added weight to her frame.

"I didn't even get your name," he said.

She turned to peer at him.

He smiled. "I'm Chris Sgro." He held out a hand and she shook it.

"Trudy. Trudy Blake."

Despite the Neapolitan she knew was melting into the bag, they continued to talk a bit. She told him about her work at the local pottery, about her boy, their dog, and what she did for fun (not much in this hellhole). He'd told her he lived in Akron, where he was an assistant professor at the University of Akron, teaching Russian literature. At the mention of that, Trudy was certain she was out of his league.

But he'd asked her out, anyway.

II

And here they were, at St. Clair's finest restaurant—Fiorello's, a little Italian joint on Mulberry Street—on their first date. Clichés filled the place—red checkered tablecloths, oil paintings of the Colosseum and the Spanish Steps, the likes of Frank Sinatra, Jerry Vale, and Rosemary Clooney playing on the sound system, and flickering, waxy pillar candles stuffed into the mouths of Chianti bottles. All these things made Trudy feel like she was in a movie like *The Godfather*.

Trudy had forgotten what being on a date felt like—what it felt like was time travel, back to when Trudy was in her early twenties and still full of hope about what a date could bring. Maybe marriage? Passionate kisses that would lead to something more? A surrogate dad for Sammy? Someone on a white horse that might sweep her and her boy up and take themselves far from this poverty-stricken area to start a new life—white picket fence, two cars in the garage, vacations—all that jazz.

That hope had been wiped out by too many drinkers, addicts, and men who thought a "yes" to an evening out automatically meant a "yes" to a romp in the sheets, even when she said no. Or men who were just plain boring—all they knew how to talk about was sports, or fishing, or hunting. Or even worse, their dead-end jobs. Or even worse than that, former wives and lovers that they either hated or couldn't seem to get over.

They never could be bothered to take an interest in

what she had to say.

The sad reality she'd come to know could be summed up in three words—*most men were pigs*. She'd yet to find a good one, the kind she watched with envy in those damned misleading holiday Hallmark movies.

But Chris, across from her, seemed like none of the men she'd experienced before. He was thoughtful and a real gentleman. He'd insisted on picking her up, opening the car door for her, and pulling her chair out at the restaurant. He'd asked if she'd mind him ordering for the both of them, and she was both relieved and delighted. Not one man in her past had ever suggested such a thing.

And what he'd ordered hadn't been disappointing, not at all. She would have ordered the same if she thought she could afford it. They'd started with calamari rings with marinara sauce, then a cup of Fiorello's incredible Italian wedding soup, followed by linguine with clam sauce. He'd ordered a bottle of white wine, the name of which she'd never heard nor could she remember, but it was delicious, just a little sweet and perfect for her palate and the food they were enjoying.

Now, as they'd finished up a shared dessert of tiramisu and coffee, Trudy was feeling very good about this date. She was also full to the brim and would have to starve herself for the next few days to not add ten pounds to her hips.

"I don't know if I can move." Trudy laughed and put a hand on her belly. "That was wonderful, but I am filled to the gills."

He chuckled and topped off her wine. "I'm glad you enjoyed. And I'm happy you have an appetite. I've gone out with too many gals who insist on 'just a salad.' I like that *you* like to eat."

"Well, considering the fact that it keeps me alive and kicking, I guess I do." She grinned. "But seriously, thank you for this. It was incredible. I don't get to enjoy stuff like this very often. The days at the pottery are so long and take so much out of me that when I get home, all I wanna do is sleep. Usually, I'm sorry to say, I end up feeling myself and Sammy tuna fish sandwiches or worse, cereal for dinner." She laughed. Warmth rose to her cheeks. "I suppose that makes me sound like a bad mother."

"Not at all. It makes you sound like a mother who works hard to take care of her son." He took a sip of wine.

"Okay," she said. "You got me. I've been resisting, but I have to be a proud mama for a minute and show you some pics of Sammy."

He leaned forward over the red-checkered tablecloth. "Oh, I want to see."

She reached down to dig in her purse to find the small photo album she carried everywhere. She brought it out and held it so Chris could see as she thumbed through its plastic sleeve pages. Here Sammy was at three on a merry-go-round at the annual St. Rocco's carnival in August; and there he was a couple of years later, looking solemn in a pressed button-down shirt, jeans, and Chuck Taylors, waiting to go inside Garfield Elementary for his first day of kindergarten. At seven, swimming at the public pool at Thompson Park, just up the hill from them. At ten, his face illuminated by the glow of a birthday cake's candles. "I always make his cakes. He loves chocolate with maple frosting. And no ice cream!

Nah, it has to be orange Jell-o." She went on to show him several school pictures—all the way up to the last one, the seventh grade class portrait.

"He's a handsome boy. Looks like you." Chris winked.

"Oh, I don't know. Probably more like his dad." She immediately regretted saying that since she knew she'd forever be uncertain about Sammy's paternity. "He's not around."

"Does he at least take an interest in the boy?"

She shook her head. "Hey, I'm out of wine." She held up her glass.

He refilled it.

And perhaps it was the wine, but she suddenly felt the urge to talk about Sammy and what she now had confirmed.

"He's gay. He just told me."

Chris leaned back, thinking. "And you're okay with that?"

Trudy was worried there would be a flaw in what seemed like the perfect man. "Of course I am. He's my boy, my heart. Who he does or doesn't love or feel attracted to makes no difference to me. I'd love him if he had three eyes and a finger for a nose." She guffawed and thought she should make this her last glass of wine. She picked up the photo album again and held it out. "The object of his affection." It was a picture of Sammy and Jeb, taken just a few days ago, as they sat on the back porch, playing Trouble.

Chris took the album from her hands and studied the picture. He then handed it back and said something that caused Trudy's heart to swell with gratitude.

"Sweet."

The one-word pronouncement brought a tear to her eye and an idea to her head. "Hey," she blurted, without pausing to think much about it. "What are you doing on the Fourth?" The holiday was coming up. Right away, she mentally scolded herself—it was too soon to be introducing Sammy to a new man. Yet he was so sweet and nice, and had no problem with him being gay.

"Nothing much. You?"

"The boys and I are going to picnic and watch them from my top-secret bluff over the river. Best viewing spot in town." She leaned forward, said *shh* and put a finger to her lips. "You can only come along if you promise not to tell anyone where it is."

He held up two fingers. "Scout's honor. Just let me know what I can bring."

"Put that thought out of your head right now. You let me treat you next time. I'll pick you up."

"Okay. Sounds great. Thanks. But please, let me do the driving. The van has more than enough room for us and whatever we bring along."

This guy is too good to be true. When's the other shoe gonna drop?

They moved on to other topics—their mutual love of dogs, which prompted Trudy to show him pictures of Vanilla; their thoughts on Ronald Reagan and his presidency and how Trudy thought he was all about the rich; favorite music, TV shows, and movies. They had so much in common.

He drove her home, walked her to her door, and gave her a chaste, closed-mouth kiss. His hands didn't roam. He didn't hint he wanted to come in. "I'll see you guys on the Fourth. Give me a buzz if you change your mind about me bringing something. I make a mean deviled egg."

He was, as he'd been all evening, a perfect gentleman.

She never saw him again.

Chapter 5

Now—Marc

"What do you do when the person you admittedly love morphs into a best friend or a roommate?

What do you do when, after many years of sharing the same bed, the same bathroom, the ups and downs of any relationship, and the endless days and nights together merge into one?

"What do you do when those days and nights no longer satisfy?

"Where do you turn?"

He wondered these things aloud, not for the first time, as he stared out the window at a leaden sky, pregnant with rain. Every so often, a strong gust of wind blew, rattling the window glass in its frames.

Sam was out grocery shopping and—more and more—Marc found he adored this time alone. It was a balm for his soul. He felt liberated, like he could breathe. It was a small taste of what it would be like to experience the greener grass—being alone.

For so long, he'd been a horse standing at a gate, gazing out over a vast empty field of green. The horse knew that if he got through the gate, there may be none of the things he possessed now—and took for granted. There would be no guarantee of a roof over his head, no regular feeding, no kind words, no loving touches. And yet...and yet... He wanted that field beyond the gate. With all its mysterious promise, freedom beckoned.

He glanced down at the phone in his hand. He'd almost forgotten he'd carried it with him when he moved to the window to check and see if the street was yet slick with rain.

A message waited for him on the hookup site, Adam4Adam. This one wasn't crude, as most were, turning him off immediately with filthy come-ons and pics of dicks and asses.

Those things had their place, but it wasn't what Marc sought.

No, this one, from a guy who called himself *IntoFreedom*, was friendly, guileless, almost naïve:

> Hey. New to the site and trying to find someone real to connect with. It's a hard task! So many flakes, so many hiding behind fake or old pics. You seemed genuine, someone who was as new to this scene as I am. I keep coming back to your picture. Handsome, sure, but there's an innocence in your eyes that holds me. So, no pressure, but just wondering if you wanted to talk more, maybe get acquainted on a personal rather than physical level (at least to start).

```
Hope you'll get back to me.
```

Marc looked away from the screen and out the window once more. The message was a turning point, one he was sure there might be no turning back.

"Should I answer? Should I cross the line in the sand?"

Almost as a reply, the sky lit up with a streak of lightning, followed by a deafening peal of thunder that caused the lights in the condo to flicker.

Chapter 6
Now—Sam

I

Two anxious weeks went by. Two weeks of nerve-tingling alarm every time the door buzzer sounded. Two weeks of restless sleep and bizarre dreams—featuring both the boy Jeb and the man who claimed to be him. Fourteen days of feeling I was being watched—on the L train heading to and from work, or at the supermarket, or when we headed out on Thursday night for comedy videos at Sidetrack on Halsted. Every time the phone rang, landline or smart, I was on edge. I didn't answer any call that wasn't clearly identified by Caller ID.

Now, though, in the humid, languorous, and waning days of August, I'd managed—somewhat—to put my strange encounter with the boy I once loved (or the one pretending to be him) out of my head. I began to breathe normally again. My heart rate and pulse slowed. I finally got around to finishing Stephen King's *Fairy Tale*, and had to credit the old boy—he still possessed the power to write engrossing, fascinating, engaging, and universal fiction—creating places I never imagined wanting to go, but then being enthralled when I got there. I started cooking again, which I'd always loved. Being so on edge the past couple of weeks had sapped my desire to create in the kitchen. We'd ended up ordering in or going out. Lucky for us, we could walk a couple of blocks over to Clark Street and have our choice of cuisines.

Today, Saturday, I'd put a chuck roast in the slow cooker, along with carrots, potatoes, pearl onions, garlic cloves and a half bottle of Cabernet. It was in the nineties outside and the idea of a roast was a couple months too soon to be proper, but what did I care? A craving was a craving. Marc was making his beer bread to go with it.

I came up behind him as he was throwing ingredients into a mixing bowl. The smell of hops was strong. I hugged him and kissed his earlobe, which made him giggle and flinch a little, raising his shoulders.

He turned to me. "What was that for?"

"Just wanted to say I love you without saying it." I eyed him. "Thanks for being so patient with me lately. I know I've been spooked, on edge, irritable, moody, and anything else you want to throw into the mix."

"No worries." Marc gave me a peck on the lips, doughy hands upraised. "Isn't that what I'm here for? To support you through the good *and* the bad?" He looked back down at his work, moving away from me slightly.

I nodded. "And I'm so grateful."

"You'll return the favor someday, hopefully in the very distant future. I doubt that creep's not coming back. It was just some kind of weird prank."

"I hope you're right. I'm beginning to feel a little better about it. Like it was a dream."

"Maybe it was." Marc used a spatula to transfer the

beer bread batter into a loaf pan. He lifted it and deposited it into the preheated oven, then wiped his hands on his shorts. "Dreams can be powerful."

I wasn't so sure about dreams, so I stole a moment by heading into the bathroom and splashing water on my face. I stared at myself in the mirror for a bit, wondering what was to become of me. Could I trust my gradually deepening gratitude that this weirdo would not return?

I decided I needed to get out, to enjoy the day, to do a little meditating, of sorts, with the sound of waves as my backdrop. I longed to be distracted.

Back in the living room, I found Marc on the couch. He was glued to an old episode of the *Barefoot Contessa*, or as I called her, the Bareback Contessa. Who knew what she and Jeffrey got up to after a nice brisket?

"Hey, I was going to take a little walk down to the lakefront. Wanna come?"

"You go." He pointed to the screen. "I love this one—it's when she invites all her handsome, gay male friends over for brunch."

"How completely out of the ordinary," I said, and we both chuckled.

"Anyway," Marc added, "I need to keep an eye on the bread. It doesn't take long and I don't want it to burn."

"Okay." I was sort of relieved. The need for some alone time was strong. I adored my husband, but even with our easy-going life, our effortless time together, the need for solitude rose up regularly, demanding attention.

Vito's pointed ears had perked up when he heard the word "walk" and now he stood at the door, stub of a tail wagging, patiently waiting to be harnessed and leashed. He most likely discerned lakefront too. That dog loved nothing more than a romp on the sand, even though it wasn't quite legal in the summertime.

Now Vito and I neared the beach. The surf roared distantly as waves crashed against the breakwater at the end of the street.

I experienced an odd sensation. A chill ran up and down my spine, and my steps faltered. Vito yanked me forward, eager to complete our trip to the beach, which I'm certain he could smell even better than I could hear.

I let myself be yanked, but couldn't shake the feeling: *Someone's watching me*. The hair on the back of my neck raised, I'm sure. I felt a cold tingle up and down my spine, even though it was hot and humid enough to put us in Louisiana.

I glanced all around and especially behind, yet saw no one out of the ordinary, no one interested in a gay man walking his smashed-in faced dog.

The tingly, unnerving sensation persisted. Intuition can be powerfully persuasive, I'd learned.

The uneasiness didn't dissipate after we crossed the beach to get to the water's edge. At least there, the crashing surface and the jewel-like sparkles on the surface of the water allayed my worry. Vito didn't care at all. I unleashed him so he could enjoy a few rapturous moments dashing through the surf, barking as if he'd reached canine Nirvana.

I was forever turning away and scanning the western horizon to see if anyone suspicious was lurking. Anyone, of course, being the guy who called himself Jeb Kleber.

My anxiety didn't ebb as Vito and I abandoned the shoreline and headed south on the lakefront trail, stopping and starting as bicyclists, runners, and rollerbladers sailed by us. Of course, Vito pulled me back many times to sniff a bush or blades of grass.

My anxiety peaked when I saw him. I got the full contingent—racing heart, sweaty palms, breathing coming in short pants, as though I'd run a marathon.

My *spidey* sense had been right all along.

Jeb sat on a park bench about a football field away. Although he held a book in his hand, he stared right at me.

Despite the heat and damp air, despite my wearing only a pair of shorts and tank top, my blood froze, leaving me cold and trembling. I wanted to turn and run, but his green-eyed stare held me in place. I was a bug pinned to an exhibition board.

Even Vito was at last unnerved, whining, and pulling at his leash, leading me in the opposite direction. It was as though he knew something wicked was about to this way come.

I listened to my dog and turned away, heading back north. My breath quickened as footsteps sounded behind, speeding up to keep pace. Only propriety kept me from breaking into a full-on sprint.

"Sammy! Can you just hold up for a minute? I know you saw me."

Several people on the trail turned to peer at me curiously. Heat rose to my cheeks.

Reluctantly, and with a sigh, I stopped in my tracks. Vito sat at my feet as though he understood my wariness and wanted to be in complete solidarity. I didn't turn around, but waited until Jeb—or whomever the hell he was—to stand before me.

We eyed each other for a moment and I hoped my fear

and anxiety weren't obvious. I didn't want him to know that he terrified me.

He spoke first. "Look, man, I just want to talk to you."

I sucked in a breath. For a moment, I feared bursting into tears. I steeled myself, drawing in a deep breath. "Why? Why? Why? That's the big theme for my questions. I have about three questions I need you to answer before I'll even begin to consider talking to you."

"Can we at least sit down?" He gestured toward one of the benches lining the trail. "Please?"

I was tempted to refuse, but conceded once I realized sitting would make it easier to keep my fear and shakiness at bay.

We settled on to the bench. I made sure to put as much distance between us as possible. Vito hopped up to occupy the space between us. He regarded Jeb with his big brown eyes and then moved a little closer, lowering his head to be petted. Jeb indulged him. I was surprised because Vito was usually extremely wary of strangers. But he'd closed his eyes in bliss at Jeb's touch.

"I just want you to know—"

I held up my hand to cut him off. "No. I don't want to hear *anything* from you until I'm satisfied about a few things."

Jeb looked out at the water and the people frolicking on the beach. He kept scratching Vito behind the ears. "Okay."

To me, those carefree folks on the beach and in the water seemed as though they were in another world. They might as well have been a million miles away or figures in some travel video.

"What can I tell you?" Jeb asked.

I looked closely at him. I could see that he could certainly *be* Jeb, all grown up. The same eyes, the same slender, wiry build. And yet there was something off. I just didn't have the intuitive feeling that this man was indeed him.

"For starters, maybe you can clue me in on why you lied about your parents." I told him how I'd spoken to my mother and what she'd said about the fate of Jeb's mother and father. "Your dad didn't pass away from lung cancer and your mom couldn't have rejected you when you 'returned.'" I put air quotes around the word returned. "Mom says they both died in a fire years ago, together. And this was *before* you said you came back to them."

He stared down at the asphalt of the path for a long time. When he looked up, his eyes glistened with tears. Even with all the weirdness of this, I felt a twinge of guilt.

"I was ashamed. They didn't just die in a fire. They were two of the biggest cooks for meth in the county. Their trailer blew up when they got careless. It's an old story, a tragic one, but also embarrassing and pathetic." He sighed and pressed a hand to first one eye and then the other. "It's not easy to admit your parents were meth heads, worse, that they cooked it and sold it. Who knows how many lives they ruined?"

I had no answer for him. I wasn't all that relieved. The story he'd given me was better, but not by much. But still, I supposed it *was* possible shame played a part in his feelings. I knew about having shame regarding a parent. I adored Trudy and appreciated the sacrifice and hard work she'd put into keeping a roof over my head, food on the table, and clothes on my back. But she'd been a promiscuous teenager when she'd had me, and I wasn't exactly proud of the fact. Sometimes, I lied about her age to acquaintances, making her older. I had, on a few occasions, even fabricated a dad who'd died heroically in his work as a police officer.

Well now, maybe I did understand, a bit, Jeb's reluctance to tell me the truth. Still, a lie is a lie. One falsehood could color every statement that came after.

"Do you get it?"

"I guess." I sighed and wished I had run away from him. But here we were, and this was my chance. And speaking of running away, I followed up with my next question. "I'm also wondering why you ran out the last time we saw each other. You didn't have to. I don't get why you'd make the time to look me up, meet me, get inside my condo, and then just slip out when I wasn't looking. It was very weird." I forced him to meet my gaze. "And suspicious."

"I don't know. I acted on impulse. See, Sammy, I wanted time to really talk to you, tell you my story, and I was freaked out when you said your husband was on his way up. I didn't want *two* people looking at me the way you were. So I left. I'm sorry. I should have said something, and I know it looks bizarre. But you have to understand, as nervous as I know you were at me appearing out of nowhere, I was even more scared. I had to psyche myself up to come to you. I didn't know how to do it. And when I was confronted with having to talk to two people when I really needed to connect with only one, I just panicked." He grinned, but it was a sad expression in spite of itself. "I'm sorry. I don't know what else to tell you. I should have handled it better and differently." He shrugged. "But I didn't. Will you give me another chance?"

The question caught me short. I didn't know. Besides, I had one more question of my own, so I ignored his and asked, "Why did you wait so long to find me?"

It was weird that at just that moment a huge bank of clouds rolled over the sun, darkening the day and making it cooler.

Jeb appeared at a loss.

I went on, "It'd been so many years, decades really. You said you were back in St. Clair fifteen years ago, at least. Why no visit in all that time? Why now?"

He didn't answer for a long time. Vito hopped down from the bench when he saw a squirrel on the grass. The dog, at least, was ready to go. And so was I. The feeling returned that this was a con man. I didn't know what he hoped to get from me, as I certainly didn't have money to spare, but this still felt all wrong. I was about ready to say so when he started talking again.

"You're not easy to find."

"What?"

"As far as I could tell, you have no presence online. No Facebook, no Twitter, no Insta or Pinterest, not even a LinkedIn. You're truly off the radar. I thought maybe you were the one who'd died."

He had a point. I'd had a MySpace page once, many years ago, and had a bad experience with a stalkerish type. I just hadn't wanted to open the door to that again. So I never jumped on the bandwagon when it seemed like everyone else in the world was doing so. "Yeah, I'm not online. But surely, there are public records you could have accessed. My phone number's never been unlisted. I pay property taxes on our condo, so there'd be a record of me online with my address." I shook my head. "Nice try, but I don't buy it." I shook my head again. "No. I can't do it."

I stood to leave. This was simply wrong. I still understood none of it, but it was time to put a stop to whatever the hell was going on. I longed for the comfort of my sanctuary, of Marc's arms, of pot roast, beer bread, and a Netflix movie watched cuddled up on the couch.

Even if this really was Jeb, and everything he said was the truth, what point was there in reconnecting *now*? I wasn't looking for a new love, a friend, an acquaintance, or anything along those lines. People change over the course of more than a quarter of a century. What could we possibly have in common today?

He peered up, not moving. "It's all true, Sammy."

I started to move away. Even Vito had had enough—he tugged at the leash, pulling me.

Jeb didn't get up. He called, "Isn't there something I can do to change your mind?" There was a pause. "I've thought about you all my life, ever since that night." He burst into tears, his breath morphing into hiccupping sobs. "Ever since he took me. Let me tell you about that."

I turned. "No. I can't. I just can't, Jeb, or whoever you are. I'm sorry if something bad happened to you all those years ago. If you really are, Jeb, I don't know how to make things right for you. I have a life, a husband, a job, and years of failures and triumphs you know nothing about. The same is true for you. It's too late."

With that, I turned and walked away.

I had to admit, though, a part of me wished he'd run after me.

But he didn't.

And yet I felt he wasn't through with me yet.

II

"Is that Sam Blake? Or are my eyes deceiving me?" The words, followed by the tinkle of feminine laughter, stopped me in my tracks on Lunt Avenue. Even Vito paused to look.

I thought of the Dorothy Parker quote, *What fresh hell is this?* I turned to see who spotted me. I just wanted to get home, and I was so close. Damn, just two more blocks, across Clark Street, and then one more block south and I'd be there.

Why was the universe trying so hard to prevent such a simple desire?

But I couldn't help but smile when I saw her. Debbie Alexander and I had worked for several years together as catalog copywriters out in Des Plaines for an office products company. The work was mind numbing and dull, but Debbie and I had bonded over our pretentious boss, Marcia Silverman, and what we thought of as her plan to make us all fat by bringing a cake in every Friday.

But since I'd been hired as an editor for one of the American Medical Association's publications down-town five years ago, she and I had lost touch. At first, we stayed connected. There was the occasional email or lunch on a Saturday, but as friendships like these tend to do, the occasions of our meeting up grew further and further apart as time intervened. Friendship withered on the vine of good intentions, as it often does.

"Debbie!" I cried. "How long has it been?" I moved toward her and we hugged. She smelled good, citrusy and clean. I leaned back to take her in. She looked great, and I told her so. "Love the new hair color." She'd gone red when before her hair had been a mousy brown, streaked through with premature gray, mostly tied back in a braid. Now it was cut short, framing her face.

"Thanks, hon." She gestured toward her tall frame, clad today in a midriff top, distressed jeans, and rhinestone-bedazzled sandals. "I did a makeover after the divorce—lost thirty pounds, more like two hundred if you count that asshole I married, got Botox, changed my hair, and now I'm living my best life here in the city."

"Wow. We've *really* been out of touch." I was actually glad I'd run into her. Her happiness at seeing me helped obliterate some of the tension I felt, erasing the need to flee. Her appearance made the world a little less creepy and threatening. She was like the sun coming out. "I didn't know about the divorce or that you'd moved from Park Ridge."

"Out of the suburbs and into life!" She laughed. "That place was suffocating me."

"And do you realize you're a five-minute walk from me?" I laughed with a bit of joy. "Girl, we need to do Friday night drinks again!"

"I didn't know until just now. But I'm thrilled! And drinks? You bet." She looked down at Vito and squatted beside him, holding her hand out a foot or so away so he could sniff if he chose. He chose and before a minute had passed, she'd won him over. Today seemed to be his day for warming to strangers. But he *had* met Debbie on a couple of occasions before. He flopped on to his belly and let her rub it, something he rarely did for people he didn't know. Much to his displeasure, she took her hand away after a minute or so and stood. "You got a little time? Wanna come up and see the place? It's just a one-bedroom, but I have a peekaboo view of the lake, if you lean the right way."

I was going to refuse, given my desire to get home. But then I glanced down at my watch and relented. The roast in the slow cooker needed at least three more hours. What was my hurry? A bit of distraction might be just the thing for getting this derailed day back on track. "I'd love that." I followed her into her high-rise building.

Debbie's apartment was tiny, but she told me the landlord had allowed her to paint it and it had a mid-century modern vibe which was really cool. Bright white walls with pops of orange everywhere—the doors, a minimalist clock on the wall, a giant hyper-realistic tangerine painting over the couch.

"You've done a fantastic job with this place." I plopped down on the couch, gratified that I had, at least somewhat, put Jeb's appearance on the lakefront trail behind. I even felt a little gaslit. Had it really even happened?

Debbie busied herself in the kitchen, but wasn't gone long. She showed up with a tray on which there was a bottle of Chardonnay, a row of water crackers, and slices of what I hoped would be a good sharp cheddar.

"You didn't have to go to this trouble." Vito obviously disagreed. He was on his hind legs, poised to sniff, if not pilfer. I shooed him away.

"Pfft. No trouble at all. Reunions should be celebrated. If I had a bottle of champagne in the fridge, I would have opened it." She sat beside me and squeezed my knee. "This is such a wonderful surprise! I'm so happy to see you."

I was touched. We toasted and got busy catching up. I told her how things were going with Marc, how my job was still boring, but being allowed to work two days a week from home made the ennui go down a lot smoother, and how long Vito had been with us. She told me about how she'd finally broken free from a cheating and emotionally abusive man, gone back to school to get an associate's degree in interior design, and how she was dating absolutely no one. "And everyone!" she added with a laugh. "Playing the field, baby. I'm just getting around to sampling the man banquet that I was pushed away from when I married that asshole when I was fresh out of high school."

It was surprising how easily a bottle of wine went down and how quickly a couple of hours had passed. But now, I really did need to get myself back home. I stood and told Debbie we'd have her over for dinner soon.

"And then drinks and dancing in Boystown?" she asked, hopeful.

"Sure, whatever you want." It had been so long since I'd had a night out like what she proposed that I almost said no. But it would be good for Marc and me to get out, to hit a dancefloor again, to admire pretty boys, sweaty and shirtless, on a crowded dance floor to a thumping techno beat. We weren't exactly old, not yet.

I hugged her, a little buzzed, leashed up Vito, and we headed out.

While we'd been inside, the sky had darkened more, with a bank of charcoal clouds moving in from the east. The wind was cooler and more intense, bringing the smell of the lake with it. Leaves rustled in the trees. Cars switched on their headlights.

A storm, or at least rain, was on the way. Maybe the idea of a roast for dinner wasn't so out-of-season after all.

Vito and I hurried toward home, the wind at our backs. The sky continued to darken.

III

Vito jumped against the condo front door, as he always did. His excitement at being home, at seeing his other daddy, never wore out. Up, down, up, down, as though his stubby legs were spring-loaded. I chuckled and made haste with the keys.

Door open, Vito rushed in, searching. He vanished from sight as he searched the condo.

"Marc?" I followed the dog, sniffing the comforting aroma of slow-cooked beef and vegetables. I was thinking of what bottle of red I'd open to go with dinner. In the kitchen, Marc's loaf of beer bread topped a cooling rack. I was happy to see he'd put in some dried herbs to enhance its homely charm even more.

I turned, examining the living room, almost expecting Marc to pop up from behind the couch. But the room was still, other than rain pelting against the windows.

It should have felt homey and warm. But it didn't. A chill ran up and down my spine.

Worry crept into my voice as I called out Marc's name again.

No response.

I went into each bedroom, peered into each of the two bathrooms. The place was deserted.

Had he run out to the store to get butter? Dessert?

We were good about checking in with each other. We always texted if we weren't where we were expected to be.

"Marc?" I called out louder, as though volume would

return my missing husband.

Vito let out a single bark and returned to stand sentry at my calves.

I reached down to scratch him behind the ears. "Where is he, boy?"

I pulled my phone from my pocket, hoping to see a text I'd missed from Marc. But there was nothing. I keyed:

> Where are you? Supper's almost ready. A little worried…

I waited, staring down at the screen, willing it to respond. After a couple of minutes, I decided I'd simply wait for him. He had to have run out on an errand, maybe believing he'd get home before I did.

I was pouring myself a glass of wine when I noticed his phone on the kitchen counter. *I guess he won't be texting back.* I laughed, but not without some uneasiness. Marc regularly forgot to take his phone with him when he went out, a source of friction for us.

This time, the sight of the iPhone, lying there so innocently, made me shiver.

"Where are you?" I wondered aloud.

I checked the slow-cooker to make sure it was now on the warm setting. I turned the oven on and set the temperature to two-hundred. I'd wrap his loaf of bread in foil and put it in there to keep warm. I checked the butter dish—there was a full stick of Kerrygold, ready to go.

I moved to the living room and sat down. The wine I'd set on the coffee table didn't look appetizing. My stomach churned and not from hunger. I told myself I was on edge because of the lakefront encounter with Jeb.

"Nothing is wrong," I said softly to myself.

The dark sky and the patter of the rain against the windows normally would have made me feel at home, cozy. Now it did the opposite.

I stood again. Vito eyed me from the chair he'd occupied opposite the couch. Perhaps it was just my imagination, but even he seemed ill at ease, worried, restless.

I rose again and moved to the window to stare outside. The rain had slowed, and the sky was an odd greenish color. The street was unusually deserted, clear of even vehicular traffic, let alone foot.

"Are you out there?" I asked. "Where?"

I tried to reason with myself. I'd only been home for fifteen minutes, maybe even less, so there was really no reason for this black shroud of dread I pulled over myself. *Everything is fine*, I tried to make myself believe. *He'll walk in the door, dripping wet, and holding our reusable shopping bag, any minute now.*

But he didn't. And as the sky darkened again, split by lightning, I turned away toward the front door.

It was then, finally then, that I noticed the crimson smear of a bloody handprint on the doorframe.

I gasped and sat down suddenly on the floor.

IV

"Honey, what is it? Why are you calling at this hour?" Sleepiness, alarm, and concern mingled in Trudy's simple questions.

I glanced at the clock on the dresser. Its blue light and blocky numbers informed me that it was a little after three a.m. I'd lain in bed for at least the last four hours, tossing and turning, knowing that if I didn't get some rest, how would I have the energy to continue the search for Marc?

"I'm sorry, Mom. I just couldn't sleep. I'm so worried. And guess what? You're the person I always turn to when life is really good to me and when it's really bad. You always listen as if I'm the most important person on earth."

"That's 'cause you are. Now, I'm assuming, because of the late hour, that nothing 'really good' has happened. Tell me right now what's going on." As she spoke, the pitch and timbre of her voice woke up, becoming more alert and more worried.

"Marc is missing." Saying the words out loud gave this conversation, appropriately, a dream's surrealism. If only...

"What do you mean?"

"He's gone." A lump formed in my throat and a couple of tears ran down my cheeks. I told her about my day, leaving out the part about seeing Jeb again because it would have been simply too much all at once. "When I got home, he was just gone."

"You say it's been about twelve hours? Is it like on TV? You need to wait twenty-four hours before making a missing persons report?"

I had left out a crucial detail. I blew out a terrified breath and told her, "I called them. They came over earlier and I gave them a report."

"I'm surprised, but glad to hear that. I have to ask: why did they bother so soon? I mean, Marc's a grown man. He hasn't been gone all that long. Is there something you're not telling me?"

Should I tell her about seeing Jeb again today? This imposter had to have something to do with Marc. I knew it in my bones.

"There is." I drew in a breath and plunged in. "There was a bloody handprint on the front doorframe. That's why the cops are taking this a little more seriously, although not as seriously as I'd like." The world collapsed around me for the umpteenth time in the past half-day and I began to sob. The fact Mom was listening made it worse. I let it all out—the terror, the loss, the worry—and choked out my grief for a good couple of minutes. At last, I pulled myself relatively together.

"Sweetie," she said and paused. In one word, I heard her agitation, her worry. "I need to come out there. I'm going to be beside myself if I don't."

I was about to protest, because that's me. But the little boy still living within me piped up in my head to cut me off. "Yeah. I'd like that."

"Okay. Listen, I'm going to let you go, okay? And I'm gonna get on the computer right now and look into flights."

"I can help you with the cost." Mom barely made ends

meet. I couldn't imagine how expensive a last-minute flight like this would be. Maybe she could get on the phone and find that rare bird—a live customer service representative who actually cared—and get a break in the price. It would be like a bereavement fare. And I immediately banished that thought for fear of cursing myself—and Marc.

"Don't worry about that right now. I'll call you back when I have something booked."

"I'll pick you up. O'Hare or Midway, doesn't matter."

She sighed. "Listen, you got enough on your plate right now. Just let your old mama worry about it all. I'll be there to help before you know it."

Her kind words were about to ignite another crying jag. "Okay," I said, a little breathless. "Hurry."

"I will. See you soon, son."

She hung up.

I turned to stare out the window. The darkness seemed to have a presence as it pressed against the glass. Like a monster...

Chapter 7

Now—Trudy

I

The Pittsburgh International Airport was nice enough, Trudy supposed. It had a franchise of one of her Pittsburgh restaurants, Primanti Brothers, which served the most amazing sandwiches she'd ever encountered.

But she wasn't hungry.

No, she was terrified.

Terrified for Sam and what might be happening to him, the danger he was in.

Terrified that danger was something for which she was partly to blame. Even though her role in Jeb's disappearance all those years ago was innocent enough and certainly lacking any bad intentions, she still clung to the guilt and shame, even after all these years.

Terrified of getting in that big silver tube and flying.

Trudy had never flown. Not once. The only place she ever really considered flying seriously was Chicago, but the fact that Sam and Marc were always willing to come back home in the summer and at holidays always made the choice easy to stay off a plane and thus, avoid risking her life in a fiery crash.

But her guilt and her protective instincts as a mother placed her at gate number 19, awaiting her flight on American Airlines to Chicago's O'Hare International Airport. Her friend Punkin had dropped her off three hours before the flight was scheduled to depart. Punkin had scoffed, "Girl, what are you gonna do with yourself for all that time? I understand wanting to get there early, but you're taking caution to a whole new level."

Punkin had tried to dissuade Trudy, telling her they could stop for breakfast across the river in Chester, West Virginia, on the way up to the airport via Route 30.

"I couldn't eat."

"Okay. Why the sudden urgency to get to Sam? Everything okay?"

Everything was definitely *not* okay. She hadn't slept for two nights. Even though she thought she was well past the age for acne, she'd broken out in pimples on her forehead and across the bridge of her nose. Somehow, even with having no appetite, she'd added five pounds to her already plump frame. She looked like shit. She felt even worse. But she didn't feel right in confiding to Punkin. Telling her friend why she was so concerned could lead to the slippery slope of admitting her culpability in Jeb Kleber's disappearance. She'd managed to keep the fact to herself now for more than three decades. Why upset the apple cart now? She breathed out a shaky sigh, keeping her eyes on the road ahead and simply said, "Hon, I just miss him, is all."

"Isn't he coming home for Thanksgiving, as usual?"

"Thanksgiving is months away! I'm just hankering for some Sammy love. I need to see him."

"So much that you're willing to clean out your savings and buy a last-minute flight?"

It was obvious Punkin wasn't buying.

That's her problem.

"Yes, yes, yes. You don't know what it's like. You never had a kid." Trudy regretted the words as soon as they came out of her mouth. Punkin's most painful memory was an abortion that went bad when she was only fifteen. The botched procedure had rendered her infertile. She made no secret of it and even joked about how much the misfortune had saved her on birth control, but Trudy knew that deep down, Punkin's heart was broken. She longed for a child with a dark and abiding passion.

She gasped when Trudy spoke, as though Trudy had struck her. "I guess I don't." With shaking hands, she lit a cigarette, quickly filling the car with smoke.

Trudy rolled down her window. "I'm sorry. I shouldn't have said that."

Punkin nodded, refusing to look at her.

They drove the rest of the way in silence, which was both a relief and a punch to the gut, amping up Trudy's nervousness about flying and what she might encounter when she got to Chicago and her son.

Punkin would get over her unkind remark. Although Trudy sincerely regretted making it.

Trudy had bigger things to worry about.

Where was her son-in-law, Marc?

What did this appearance of the imposter—he just had to be—calling himself Jeb mean?

Were the two, as she strongly suspected, related?

Despite the coldness in the car and the lack of conversation, Punkin hugged Trudy and kissed her when she dropped her off at the American entrance at arrivals. "You be careful, sweet lady. I couldn't bear if anything happened to you. You're all I have."

Trudy was touched at how Punkin got a little breathless and the shimmer in her brown eyes. She touched her friend's face for a moment and then hopped from the car.

II

Trudy was okay as long as they were on the ground. From her window seat near the rear of the plane, she watched as they loaded the luggage. She eavesdropped on the flight attendants' conversations as they prepared for flight in the galley space behind her. She watched everyone come on board, certain they all had to be more matter-of-fact about flying than she. No one else's heart was pounding. No one else's palms were sweating. It was Trudy and only Trudy who was scared out of her wits, as she told her paranoid self.

But once the plane began moving, gathering speed as it taxied down the runway, she found it hard to even draw breath. As the plane jerked and began its ascent, she clung to the seat rests so hard her fingertips went pure white.

"Easy," said the older woman next to her. She was a grandmotherly type, reminding Trudy of the Jean Smart grandmother in the television miniseries, *Dirty John*. She had the same kind face, the same bubble of teased and shellacked gray hair. She even wore what Jean's character in the movie would have—a beige sweater set and neatly pressed white slacks with low heels in beige.

"First time?" The woman regarded her through her big round frames, concern in her hazel eyes.

Trudy, heart in throat, only nodded.

The woman patted her hand. "Just lean back. Close your eyes. Take a few deep breaths. In with the serenity, out with the fear—slowly."

Trudy did as the woman told her, partly as a way to thank her for her kindness to a stranger and partly because she hoped the advice would work.

And it did—to a point. She kept her eyes closed, deep breathing, until there was an announcement that they'd reached cruising altitude, whatever the hell that meant. Her breath came a little easier, but her heart continued to pound at an accelerated rate. She turned to look at her savior. "Thanks for that. I probably would have totally lost it if it weren't for you." Trudy managed a smile.

The woman smiled back. "It's okay, sweetie. It wasn't that long ago I was in your shoes." She chuckled. "Didn't get on a plane until I was sixty-two. That's when my son got the job in Chicago, at Leo Burnett. That's a big ad agency. He's a brilliant designer and Pittsburgh just got too small for him." She took out a roll of Lifesavers and offered one to Trudy. "I'm Lizzie, by the way."

Trudy took a Lifesaver and popped it into her mouth. "Trudy. I'm going to see my son, too."

"This your first trip to Chicago?"

Trudy nodded. They continued to chat about where their sons lived in the city, about what Trudy should see while she was there, about the ages of their sons and their marriages. Lizzie was delighted to learn that Sam had a husband. Her son, Ryan, did too. Both couples had dogs.

Lizzie, thankfully, never asked about the reason Trudy was making the trip. Trudy supposed she simply assumed she missed her son and wanted to see him, as Lizzie herself did.

Toward the last twenty minutes or so of the flight,

Trudy actually experienced her body letting go of tension, not completely, but the stress from the flight markedly abated. She closed her eyes for what she thought would be a moment.

She's in the woods and Jeb tramps through the soft padding of fallen leaves and dirt ahead of her. The moon shines down, giving a sort of silver glow to everything, as if these moments were filmed in black and white by some old-time director from the 1940s.

"Jeb, honey, wait up!" Trudy calls in what she thinks of as a loud voice, a shout in the empty darkness. But what comes out is just above a whisper, barely audible to her own ears.

Jeb obviously doesn't hear. He quickens his pace.

And then Trudy opens her mouth to scream, yet no sound emerges.

Hands emerge from the shadows, from behind the barks of trees lining the path. They snatch Jeb away, right off his feet. There one moment and gone the next...

Trudy stops in her tracks, stunned and terrified. She jumps at the boom of a firework in the distance. It's like thunder.

She waits, hoping Jeb will return. Hoping something will happen so she can intervene and save him from what she knows will be decades of missing-in-action.

But he never does.

And as Trudy stands, still as a statue, the sky lightens from dark blue, to gray, to orange, until finally—full daylight.

She can't move.

At last someone does *emerge from the woods. But it's*

not Jeb.

It's Chris Sgro. He's smiling. In his hands, he holds out a honeydew melon. But there's a knife stuck in it and blood seeps from the 'wound.'

Trudy screams and screams.

The impact of landing jolted her awake all at once. She struggled to get herself in a more upright position, disoriented and a little nauseated. The sky outside was milky white.

Lizzie looked at her with a little fear, but more concern. "Bad dream, hon?"

Trudy sighed, grateful to be back in reality, even if it was on a plane. "Yes. A doozie." She wasn't about to go into detail.

"You screamed a bit there. A weird moan, kinda muffled, but alarming all the same." Lizzy patted her hand. "You're back amongst the living now—and safe."

Trudy wished that were true. Oh, how she wished it.

The plane taxied toward the gate, and at last, they stopped. There was an announcement about the weather in Chicago and how passengers could now take their phones out of airplane mode and use them. Trudy did so, shooting Sam a quick text—I'm here!

Her only thought: *soon, I'll be reunited with Sam*. The thought was both welcome and terrifying. She wished there was a happier reason for her travel. Could she be the mother she wanted to be? The one who could make everything all right?

She smiled helplessly at Lizzie and thanked her once more for her kindness.

III

The L train ride, long and crowded as it was, was not as terrifying as the plane. *At least we're on terra firma!*

Before they parted at the gate, Lizzie explained how to get to Sam's apartment in Rogers Park. "Now you could take a cab. That's the easiest, but, honey, it'll cost you an arm and a leg! What you want to do is just follow the signs for the train into the city. Buy a pass before you go down to the platform from one of the kiosks. It'll only cost you a couple bucks, and it could very well be faster than a cab, depending on traffic—and traffic is always bad. Here at O'Hare, the train is the blue line, which will get you downtown, but not to Rogers Park."

Lizzie caught Trudy's look of fear. "Now, don't you worry. It's easy. Take the blue line downtown to Roosevelt. You'll be in the subway. Just get out and follow the signs for the red line trains. You'll have to go through a tunnel and up a flight of stairs, but the signs will guide you. Once you're on the red line, going north—the sign on the front of the train will say Howard, for Howard Street, at the end of the line. You just take that all the way up to Morse Avenue, okay?"

"Sounds complicated."

Lizzie grasped her hands. "Honey, it's *not*. You'll see. I'd come with you, but my end of the line is downtown. My boy and his husband live in Printers' Row. Plus, I need to grab a bite; I'm starving. You'll do just fine. The signs will guide you."

Trudy hoped so. She squeezed Lizzie's hands back

and then let go. "Thanks a lot. You're an angel." And she meant it.

Now, as the second train in her journey rumbled north, rising up out of the subway into the overcast summer day, Trudy was amazed at the difference. The moving from darkness into light awed her. She tried to take in all the cross streets whizzing by below her, the backs of brick apartment buildings with their wooden porches and stairs. She eyed the apartment windows, so close to the tracks, and wondered how people could live in those places. The noise alone would drive her crazy. *And wouldn't people be looking in my windows at all hours of the day and night?* As she had the thought, the train stopped for a moment and she saw a man in white briefs stirring something while standing at a stove, a cigarette dangling from his lips.

Before long, the speaker announced that Morse was the next stop. Sam had told her to "walk west to Wolcott Avenue and then walk north to Lunt." She would have asked him to give her the directions in 'normal person' language, one that didn't require an innate sense of geography.

Thank God for smartphones.

She descended the stairs after disembarking from the train, feeling as though her nerves were scraped raw by all the smells, sounds, and people. Already, she needed a break from the riot of people pressed so close, such busy, busy people. Where were they all going? Outside the station, the sidewalk was littered with trash. Cars crept in both directions on Morse Avenue, perfuming the air with their exhaust. Ethnic restaurants, bars, electronics stores, and apartments buildings crowded the edge of the sidewalks.

She leaned against the brick façade of a storefront advertising cigarettes, beer, and lottery tickets (life's three essentials) to bring up Google Maps on her phone. She keyed in her son's address and got walking directions to his place. It was a little under a mile, but with the heat and oppressive humidity, she knew she's be drenched with sweat by the time she reached Sam's front door.

She hoped only she didn't smell bad.

This would be the most exercise she'd had in years. She chuckled at the thought and started off, hoping no one would mug or murder her.

IV

Sam's building was lovely. A white brick U-shape with a courtyard in the middle, it radiated calm and peace, in opposition to her nerves. Three mature maple trees stood in the center of the courtyard. At their base, daisies grew, a bright white and yellow profusion. Near-by, a bench offered rest and a place to meditate.

She located his entrance and the apartment number on the intercom mounted on the door frame.

She took a deep breath. She needed courage. This vis-it was not only to a traumatized son, it was to someone for whom she'd repressed her guilt and shame for so many years, it was as much a part of her as her limbs.

And today, she planned to break the seal on her secret. *Will it be a relief? Or will Sam never speak to me again?*

It was a huge gamble.

Hand trembling, she pressed the intercom button.

Chapter 8
Now—Sam

I

When the intercom buzzer sounded, it was as though I'd awakened from the dead. Head pounding, limbs heavy, and eyelids scratchy, I suddenly recalled what was important about this day. Mom was coming to Chicago—for the first time—yet I lacked even a smidgen of energy to do anything about her arrival. I'd spent so much time over the last few days, since Marc had vanished, to do anything to get ready for what should have been an important moment. I'd left a towering mound of dishes, cups, glasses, and flatware in the sink, tempting a roach invasion. The coffee table was littered with a thick layer of dust, half-empty Giordano's pizza boxes, and half-drunk cans of soda. I'd discarded clothes in every room except, oddly, the bath, which now sported a carpet of damp towels, probably pregnant with mold. She looked fearful, but I thought that was understandable under the circumstances. "Right this way." I moved toward the hallway.

Trudy would be appalled. And I couldn't blame her.

Growing up, our house was tiny and decrepit, but my mom had always been a stickler about keeping it spotless. With her around, not even a dust mote had much hope for survival.

But at least that sharp metallic bark, heralding her arrival, got me off my bed and its sweaty sheets.

Curiously, I had no shame at the state of the apartment. What would have been worse would have been a super-tidy home, as though I cared more about cleanliness than where my missing spouse was.

A quick look in the mirror by the front door revealed someone at least a decade older—bags under my eyes almost like bruises, hair greasy and stringy, T-shirt stained and smelly, a pair of sweat shorts with a ragged hole near my left thigh. It was almost as though I'd tried to create a portrait of despair and succeeded.

When I opened the door, the look of shock and dismay on her face was apparent. She took a step back and then, grinning, corrected herself. She brushed by me. "You stink."

"Hello. And welcome to you, too."

I trudged along behind her as she dragged her rolling suitcase into the living room. She threw one of my shirts off the recliner in the corner and plopped down. She didn't say a word, not for the longest time, but her expression spoke volumes. Her lips turned down more and more, the lower one trembling. Her greenish brown eyes welled and became glossy with tears.

The best she could do was mutter, "Oh, Sammy."

We faced each other for a long while until at last she rose and held out her arms. I'd never seen a more comforting or welcoming sight, proving to me that we all stay children in our hearts when we're around a caring parent. I all but collapsed into her embrace. We sobbed, clinging to the other.

The comfort and the hug seemed to last forever, but it was actually only for a couple of minutes.

At last, Trudy pulled away, sniffling and gasping for air. She rubbed at her eyes, smearing mascara so she looked like a raccoon, but I couldn't bring myself to laugh.

"Are you okay?" she asked in a trembling voice.

"Sit back down."

She did, and I grabbed a seat on the couch. "No," I said. "Of course not. The world is now a nightmare. I keep hoping I'll wake up and everything will be back to boring normal. I'm longing for boring normal, Ma, like it's a place. I want it all back, though—Marc, never to have seen this guy who calls himself Jeb. I'm desperate for a do-over of the day I took the dog to the beach. I don't want to run into Jeb again. And I don't want to come home to an empty apartment and a bloody handprint on the front doorframe." I nodded to the door, indicating the print. It was still there, faded to a dark rust color, a ghost of a crime.

At mention of the dog, Vito lifted his head. He lay at my feet, perhaps even more abject than I was. Although he probably didn't understand the details of all that had transpired recently, he took his cues from me and also from Marc's absence. He reflected back my trauma and longing. I could barely get the poor dog to eat, no matter what treats—chicken, steak, carrots—I put down for him. He rarely left my side. And when he did, it was because he heard a noise outside the condo—someone traipsing up the stairs, a delivery downstairs, a burst of music when someone opened or closed their door—and he'd run to the front door, tail wagging, expecting, I was certain, to see Marc. He'd jump up and down, nails scratching at the door and when I finally gave in to his excitement and opened it, his heart would break every time at the sight of the empty hallway.

"What can I do? Give me something." Mom, for once, seemed lost and helpless, smaller somehow. She leaned forward and peered at me. "You hungry? I could make you something to eat. A sandwich?"

"Ah, spoken like a true mama." I smiled, but the expression was weak, uncertain. "There's probably nothing to make, even if I did have an appetite." I stood. "The one clean room in the house is the guest bedroom, but only because I haven't been in there. Why don't we get you settled?"

"Okay." Trudy got up to follow. "I think, under the mess, you have a very nice place, sweetheart. I hope you'll allow me to tidy up."

"I know I can't refuse, not with you." I smiled. "We'll sort something out to eat after you unpack. There's a little Mexican place around the corner on Clark; you'll love it. Burritos the size of your head." I spoke the words, even though my very empty stomach churned at the thought of food. But feeding my mother would give us both something to do, a place to be.

"And then, when we get back, you're gonna allow me to clean this place up." She eyed him pointedly. "And then we can have a good talk."

II

We got back to the condo just in time. Over the course of our meal, we hadn't said much beyond the pleasantries, skirting the trauma and horror of what my life had become over the course of just a few days. We also avoided eating more than a few bites. Predictably, neither of us had much of an appetite, although Mom managed to at least finish an enchilada.

Neither of us had sangria or a margarita. Somehow, drinking felt wrong.

We walked back in silence, other than noting how the temperature had dropped while we were inside Rosa's Cocina. A fishy-smelling wind had blown up, skimming the surface of Lake Michigan to the east and wiping out the humidity and heat of the past several days. A flash of heat lightning on the horizon told me rain was imminent.

The storm arrived just as we got in the front door downstairs. The rain came down in lashes, a deluge that turned the evening outside gray and opaque.

We hurried upstairs, where Mom got into her pajamas and made us tea. "Glad to see you have Constant Comment," she called from the kitchen. "It's my favorite."

I said nothing and busied myself with trying to tidy up the living room for us. I succeeded mainly in shoving all the discarded clothing into a pile in a corner. It was too much effort to put it into the bathroom hamper, let alone the washing machine. I slid some of the boxes and cans to one side of the coffee table to make room for the mugs.

Once we had our tea, steaming, in front of us, we both knew the time had come for us to talk. I sipped the tea, its spicy citrus scent actually enticing me a bit. "There's not much to tell you, Ma. Four days ago, I came home from walking Vito down at the lakefront and he was gone. The only trace he'd left was the handprint." I bowed my head. I couldn't bear to look at it again, nor to acknowledge it in any way.

"You talked to the police?"

"Of course. At first, they wouldn't even listen to me. A middle-aged gay man turns up missing?" I shrugged. "I guess it happens every day around these parts. After a couple days, they took me a little more seriously, even assigned a detective to the case after I filed a report, but I could tell there wasn't much urgency. Marc's disappearance was low priority. I don't know if it was because we're gay, or because we're older, or because we're in a long-term marriage, but I suspect they simply thought Marc left me."

As I spoke the words, I felt an uncomfortable twinge in my gut as I had an epiphany.

Had he left me? Could it be as simple as that? The only thing I'm sure was gone was him.

His phone is here. I keep it charged, but very little has come through. We had separate closets and Marc had a lot of clothes. I supposed he could have grabbed an old suitcase and taken some things and I might not have noticed. It wasn't like I had an inventory. And what if he had one of those—what do you call it—burner phones? And what if—and this notion was as disturbing as it was reassuring—what if the bloody handprint was tied to something as innocuous as he'd cut himself before leaving? A simple kitchen accident...

I looked up to find Mom studying my face. "What's going on in there?" She tapped her own forehead.

I told her. We both paused to peer out at the rain pouring down the windowpanes. The distant rumble of thunder informed us the rain would be with us for a while.

"He wouldn't just leave you, honey! I've known Marc almost as long as you have. He doesn't have it in him."

In spite of her pronouncement, Mom didn't know him as *well* as I did. She'd been around him only when we'd gone back home to St. Clair for holidays, times when we were mostly happy and in sync. We were always together, Marc and I, during those times. Mom rarely, if ever, had a chance to speak to him alone, let alone talk about anything of substance.

I'd never shared with her what had really evolved over the past few years. The facts were embarrassing and, in a way they shouldn't have, shamed me.

And that truth, which I wasn't ready to give space outside my own mind, was that we had grown bored with each other. Not so much me, but definitely him. I could tell from the distracted look on his face when I spoke with him and how he often missed hearing me completely because his mind was elsewhere.

Our lives, if I was honest, had become routine, lacking in passion or joy. We hadn't had sex in two years at least. We were, at best, companionable roommates, settled in our daily meals, TV-watching, and going to bed earlier and earlier.

Maybe Marc had simply had enough. I knew, in my darkest moments, I'd fantasized about what life would be like without him and, in those moments, being on my own had its appeal, even if it did bring up a hot rush of guilt. Perhaps he was having the same fantasies and one day, when the most exciting event was beef stew for dinner, he'd decided to chuck it all and start over somewhere new. Maybe even with someone new?

But Marc wouldn't just walk out, would he? Wouldn't we talk? Make a plan? See a marriage counselor or at least a divorce lawyer?

The sad truth: we don't ever really know what goes on in the minds of those we love. Not really.

One thing I *did* know about my husband—he had a fear of confrontation bordering on the irrational. If I faced the sad facts of life, it was this: he could sneak out when I was gone, simply to avoid what might come after—the arguments and the tears. Leaving may have just been easier, despite how cowardly it was.

Is this all that had happened? Something so, so—mundane?

"Ma, I don't know. I don't have your confidence."

"Why? Were you two having problems?"

"No, not really. We never fought."

"Well, then, there you go. Why would a man leave a handsome guy and a marriage where you got along so well?"

"We *never* fought, Ma. I don't know if that's such a good sign." I took a breath, debating whether I should make my next admission, especially to my mom. In the end, I decided she needed the truth. "We never make love either, not anymore. Things had become rote, painfully dull, if you want the truth."

"Oh sweetie, that happens a lot to married people

who've been together for a long time. You come to appreciate the company, the traditions, the sense of family. Sometimes, lust is the first thing to go. I'm not convinced."

"I wish *I* was." Suddenly, the notion of him simply running away was taking on more and more credence. If that *were* the case, I was sure he'd be in touch at some point in the near future. I knew he couldn't be so heartless as to worry me this way.

"Maybe it was that Jeb person, or the guy pretending to be him? Maybe he snatched him?" Worry creased her features.

"No. I saw him, even spoke with him, at the time Marc went missing."

"Well, maybe he was in cahoots with someone? Was he deliberately delaying you at the beach so this could happen?"

"I suppose that's possible."

But was it? I thought of Occam's Razor, which said something along the lines of once you remove unnecessary information, what remained was the truth. Marc being yanked out of our home was fantastic, the stuff of thriller books and movies, but wasn't it more likely he, like many other men, simply walked away from life as a result of ennui and a middle-aged crisis? I mean, we weren't rich or celebrities. We were just ordinary, liberal, middle-class gay men. There was no reason for anyone to kidnap either of us, or worse. What would they stand to gain? I sighed. "But I don't know."

The rain had abated, slowing to soft taps on the window. With its slowing down, the thunder and lightning went back to wherever they'd come from. We sat in silence for a while. I wasn't sure what more I could tell her.

"Maybe we should both try to get some sleep?" For the first time, I felt like I actually could. I was weary to my bones.

Mom nodded. "But before we do, there's something I have to tell you." She sucked in a breath and I saw something—maybe fear or worry—light up her eyes.

"What do you mean?"

She licked her lips. Wiped a hand across her face. Sipped her tea. Looked once more out the window. The patter of the rain was eerie, unsettling. It made me think of swimming in the Ohio all those years with Jeb and the summer storm that prompted us to swim back from a tree-covered island.

"Ma?"

"I know. I know. This is hard." She rose and went to the window. I couldn't imagine what was so fascinating out there, unless avoidance stood on the corner, leaning against the STOP sign.

Without turning back to me or returning to her seat, she began to talk. "Remember when Jeb vanished? That night in the woods?"

"Of course I do." Sadly, that night could have happened yesterday instead of three decades ago. The details of it were seared into my memory, as though the soft pink tissue of my brain had been branded with exploding fireworks and deep forest shadows. I doubt there was even a single detail I'd forgotten.

She said nothing for the longest time. I had to prompt her again.

She turned away from the window, revealing a face

that was a mask of fear and pain. "I don't know how to say this." She sat on the couch, gnawing her lower lip.

"What is it? Just come out with it, Mom. There's nothing you can say that will change my love for you."

After a long silence, one in which I considering giving up and simply suggesting we go to bed. We could talk in the morning.

At last, the words burst out of her. It was like a dam breaking. She spoke fast, almost as though she knew if she didn't, she couldn't reveal what plagued her. "I might have had something to do with what happened. I didn't mean to, honey, I never meant to, but I could have helped set this nightmare in motion." Her breath hitched. She was near tears. She lowered her face into her hands.

I reached over to massage her shoulder and then let go. "What is it? I know you couldn't have possibly done anything on purpose that would have caused Jeb's disappearance. That's impossible. Unimaginable."

She revealed her tear-stained face. The sadness there dug deep into my heart. "I know, I know. But I can't help but worry something I did back then might have led to Jeb being taken."

"What are you talking about? This makes no sense."

"Remember Chris Sgro?"

I shook my head. The name meant nothing.

"I went out with him around that time. Only once, though. You never met him."

"Mom, you went out with lots of guys. How am I supposed to remember someone you went out with once thirty-odd years ago?"

"Well, I've never forgotten him." She drew in a quivering breath. "Because he may be the culprit." A quivering breath, verging on a sob, emerged. "He took him. I'm sure of it."

I was dumbfounded. "No." I scratched my head. "What makes you say that? And even if you have suspicions, how can you be sure?"

"Because I invited him to come along with us to watch the fireworks. I told him where we'd be. Our secret spot."

"Oh Mom, that doesn't mean anything."

"No? Think again, because I'm pretty sure it does. *Did* he come with us, as we planned? No. When we parted after our date, he promised he'd pick us up in his van, told me he'd even bring food, yet he never showed up. I was too embarrassed to say anything to you at the time. I just thought I'd been stood up. *Not* big news for me back in those days." She stared down at the floor and then looked up again. "Everything he told me was a lie. He said he had family in the area. He didn't. He told me he came back to, I think, take care of a sick parent. None of it panned out. I know. I checked into it. All I found was that no one had ever heard of him. It was almost as though he was a ghost, someone who'd never existed."

The darkness pressed in at the windows like an alien presence. "Wait."

"I'm so sorry," she blurted.

"Wait," I repeated. "You knew all this back then and you're just mentioning it now?"

She couldn't look at me. She drew her legs up toward her chest and turned away. The move should have made her look girlish, but all I saw was an old woman, overweight, with roots that needed a touch-up. In that moment, she was a stranger—one I hated.

She went on. "I was so ashamed. I tried to convince myself it didn't matter. I told myself I'd only met the guy once and everything he told me was a lie. So, what good would it have done to report it, except for making me look partially responsible, even if what I did was totally innocent?"

I shook my head. I knew she had a point. And, of course, I didn't hate her. She was my mom and she'd lived her whole life practically in service of me, using her meager means to make sure I had everything I needed and wanted. She went without so I could have. And her reasoning made sense. But it also twisted my gut into knots with all the what ifs that arose. If she'd told me or, especially, informed the police, it could have helped.

Perhaps.

"Maybe he had nothing to do with it," I offered, feeling horrible for her. To have carried this secret around for so long must have been like a cancer on her soul.

"Of course he did. No one knew about our spot. Remember? We were so proud of our secret place." She paused a minute, breath coming more quickly. "I actually showed him a picture of you two. He must have been waiting in the woods and when Jeb went back in there to pee that night—" She began to cry, her chest heaving, wracking sobs that threatened to steal her breath. "He was like a spider in a web, waiting to pounce."

I sighed; her spider image chilled me to my core. I had no choice but to wrap my arms around her, to comfort, even though I felt at odds with my emotions. I couldn't decide whether to be furious or sympathetic.

After all, something very bad happened that she might well have made possible, even unwittingly.

Oh God.

Now, I wanted the man who called himself Jeb to show up just one more time, if only to see what he knew about what my own mother had just told me.

After a long while, I could practically feel the shame, the guilt, and the self-loathing emanating off her like an odor. I imagined all the years she must have tortured herself, the punishment she must have meted out on her own head for decades. Carrying something like that around couldn't have been good for her health—physical or mental.

"Mom, oh Mom," I said, knowing she needed reassurance, which was only mine to give. "You couldn't have possibly known. You couldn't have had a clue. When he didn't show up, you must have just thought you'd gotten unlucky with yet another man. I'm sure it didn't occur to you that he was a predator or something horrible like that."

"No. It never did." She relaxed, but only a little. "Of course it never did." She sat quietly for a while; she was thinking, wringing her hands. "I did try to follow up in the time after Jeb disappeared. Back then, there was no social media, so I had to learn to use the library and I searched property records. There was only one family in the whole area with the odd surname of Sgro and they were down the river, in Wellsville. I went to see them, and found an older woman, Kate, living with her mother in a big old house on the riverfront." She shook her head. "They knew nothing. Never heard of Chris or Christopher, or whatever. The mother had come over from Sicily as a young girl, for an arranged marriage to a man who would die a few short years later. Most of their people remained in Sicily. It was a dead end. And so was me going around and talking—discreetly—to as many folks as I could.

"He was a ghost, I tell you. No one saw him. Hell, maybe that wasn't even his real name."

The exhaustion caught up with me all at once. It was as though it had been hiding in the wings these past few days. Having Mom here and trying to absorb her shocking revelation left me utterly drained. "I need to sleep."

She nodded. "I understand. I'm worn out too."

Neither of us made a move to go to our respective bedrooms. I think it was because she wanted to know I didn't hold her innocent transgression against her.

She said, "Can you ever forgive me, Sammy?" Tears glistened in her eyes.

I stood, and she followed suit. I took her in my arms and whispered. "I already have. I love you." I meant the words, although to be honest, I hadn't completely absorbed them. "Now, you need to forgive yourself, okay?"

She pulled back, a sad smile raising the corners of her lips. "Thank you," came out as little more than a sad whisper.

"We should both get some sleep."

And this time we did head in the direction of beds and pillows. Just before she went into the guest room, I said, "Things are different now, what with the internet and all. Maybe we can find something out in the morning."

"Maybe. Wouldn't that be somethin'?"

I went into my room and closed the door behind me.

The room, lit only by the nightlight I'd plugged into a wall socket, was a dark comfort and a taunt, both at once.

Marc should have been there, on the bed, his pillow propping up his head as he read a chapter from whatever book he was engrossed in. John Boyne, maybe?

But the emptiness of the bedroom made me feel both alone and lonely, two very different things. I snapped my fingers to tell Vito to hop up onto the bed. He did and then settled near Marc's pillow, probably drawn by the lingering scent of him.

I undressed quickly, dropping my clothes to the floor under Vito's watchful eye. I knew he was waiting for me to get under the covers, so he could burrow beneath the sheet and quilt and curl up next to me. It was routine, and I figured routine was more important than ever for the little guy.

I crawled into bed and waited until his warmth was flush against my own.

Just as I was drifting off, my phone sounded, indicating a text message coming through. I debated on just leaving it until the morning, but then I realized something. I had DO NOT DISTURB mode enabled, which meant other than Marc, Mom, and my boss at work, no one could really get through to me until 7 am.

I sighed, knowing it wasn't Mom. Unlikely that work would be calling, too. I rolled over and snatched up the infernal thing off the nightstand.

What I saw there at first confused me, because I didn't recognize the number. How would such a call come through? It was a 773 area code, so at least I knew it was from the northside of Chicago.

```
Hey, it's me. I'm so sorry to worry
you. I know my absence must be
making you crazy and worse, scared.
Don't be. I can't say much more
right now other than I'm okay. And
I will be okay. I need some time. To
think. To reevaluate. To determine
where the rest of my life should
go.
Please understand.
Love, M.
```

I dropped the phone to the bed. I had questions. Since there was a number attached to the text, I tried calling it back.

Nothing. Just an automated voice with a generic, no-name message. Anyone could have sent it, right?

But why would they?

Why would they hint at midlife crises and time to think? Those reflected my thoughts and fears from earlier.

I set the phone back down and rolled over, tried to sleep.

I was in those woods again. Jeb had just left to go pee. I wasn't yet concerned.

And why should I be? Here he was now, coming back to me.

A firecracker went off somewhere in the distance. Even though the sound was dampened, it startled me.

Mom was busy packing up and Jeb surprised me. He took me in his arms and kissed me.

When he pulled away. I stared into his eyes, the moonlight reflected in them. I traced the contours of his face with my fingers.

"I love these." I fingered the small moles he had just below his lower lip, on his chin. "Sexy."

And then I woke. A glance at the clock across the room told me it was 3 am. Vito snored on Marc's pillow beside me.

I grabbed my phone, searching for Marc's text message, but the last message on there was from Mom, alerting me to her arrival at O'Hare. I set the phone back down, relieved and disappointed.

I sat up a bit, leaning against the headboard. I knew the rest of the night, sleep would elude me.

Lying there, I searched my memory.

Had the man who'd called himself Jeb had two moles on his chin?

III

We stood on the Blue Line L platform at its terminus—O'Hare Airport. People hurried to and from the airport proper all around us. Trains chugged, waiting, in the gray and uninspiring station. Mom's three-day visit had been worthwhile, but far too brief.

"I wish I could stay longer, honey, but I'll lose my job."

I followed her up the escalator and into the airport proper.

I hated that she couldn't get away for more time from the industrial pottery where she worked. She'd been there so many years, working herself quite literally to the bone, and they couldn't even give her some kind of compassionate leave. I hated even more that this first-ever visit to me in Chicago had to be cut short, especially since she'd stepped out of her comfort zone and flew for the first time in her life. It was a bigger step than she'd allow herself credit for.

But I knew the realities of her work—piece work labor. Despite hard, thankless work that drained her, she could be replaced in the blink of an eye if she challenged the pottery's rules. In St. Clair and the surrounding areas, jobs like hers were hard to come by. Once upon a time, the place was heavy with industry, steel and pottery mostly, but those were bygone times and had been since before I was even born.

"I know, I know. The fact that you overcame your fears to come out here and support me means more than I can say. It really did help—just being here made me feel less alone with my fears." I drew in a shaky breath. "Nothing compares to a mother's love, even when you're an old fart like me."

Mom rolled her eyes. "You're hardly old, honey. If you're old, what does that make me? Ancient?"

Travelers hurried around us. We were a small island in a human stream.

"Well, I hardly did anything." She toyed with the handle on her roller bag.

"Stop. You did a lot. You made me feel supported and even allowed me to hope a little. And you gave me a name that might lead somewhere." I shrugged. "Who knows? This whole thing is just unreal."

She hugged me too hard, but I didn't mind. "I really need to get to my gate."

I chuckled. "Your flight doesn't leave for two hours and you're already here. Relax."

"I know, I know, but I worry. Please try to understand."

And I could see she really was concerned about being on time. Her fear was irrational, but I understood.

"You'll call that private investigator we found?"

We'd looked up a few private investigators the day before yesterday and vetted them on Yelp, thinking someone with better internet and access to other resources might help us locate who this Chris Sgro person was. I knew, even if we found him, it could lead to another dead end, and certainly might not help us find Marc. My funds were severely limited, so it's not like I could use someone for very long.

"I will. I'll call her as soon as I get home. And I'll let you know what she says."

"Good deal."

We hugged again, pecked each other's lips. I was genuinely sad and distressed to see her go. From her forlorn expression, I knew the feeling was mutual.

As she started away, I called to her, "Wait."

She paused and turned toward me.

"I meant to ask you and keep forgetting. Do you still have that photo you took of Jeb and me that summer?" I could still see it in my mind's eye, tucked into the small photo album Mom used to take everywhere with her, before the advent of smart phones and the ability to take not just a dozen snapshots everywhere, but thousands. Jeb and I were on our little back porch in the redwood chairs with their floral pattern cushions. We both had looked annoyed because she'd interrupted our game of Trouble. I wished I'd held on to that picture; it was the only one of the two of us.

She cocked her head. "From all those years ago? I don't know, but I'll take a look when I get back. If I find it, I can ask Judy Cope next door if she can scan it with her printer and then I can just email it."

I was surprised by my mom's ingenuity and technical know-how; it hadn't even occurred to me to ask her to simply scan the photo. But the picture itself? It was most likely long gone. Over the years, Mom had moved several times and with each time, there was an unburdening. Now, in a one-bedroom downtown that leased to its tenants based on income, she had even less space for mementos. Still, maybe she'd hung onto it, knowing its link to such a traumatic event in our lives.

"That would be great."

"No promises." She started away again. "But I'll look as soon as I get home." She stared longingly at the sign for security. "If I get home..." she started off again. Her worries were kind of cute in a way, but I hated to interrupt her forward momentum again.

"One more thing." She stopped and let out a frustrated sigh. There was no way in hell she'd miss her flight, even if the line for security was long, but try telling her that.

"Do you remember what Jeb looked like?"

"Yeah, pretty much, but hon, that was ages ago. And I'm getting to that stage where I go into a room and forget why." She laughed.

"One little thing. Do you recall if he had a couple moles on his face?"

My heart sunk when she rolled her eyes. "Seriously? That was thirty-some years ago. I don't remember what we had for lunch yesterday." She moved toward me and smooshed my cheeks. "I know you're doing your due diligence by asking. You'd remember better than I would."

This time, she turned and left for good. I watched as she disappeared among O'Hare's throngs of travelers.

I stood for a while, waiting. I searched my memory for the face of the man who called himself Jeb and couldn't recall for sure if he had those same moles. I didn't think so, but again, I wasn't sure.

IV

I went with Harriet McGill because her website said she specialized in missing people and, more importantly, that she could work with aliases. That piece of information might have been a benefit for all private investigators these days, but she was the only one that advertised it on her website. And that function could come in extremely useful, especially if all it involved was plugging the name Chris Sgro, or a variation of it, into an online database.

I called her and was surprised that she could meet with me the next afternoon after I got off work.

So now I found myself on the Purple line L train, on my way to downtown Evanston, where Harriet's office was located. I imagined entering a rundown office building with no elevator. Her office would have a frosted glass window with her name etched on it. Inside, there'd be a hat and coat rack and a battered metal desk, seen through a haze of cigarette smoke.

I had watched too many noir movies.

I walked from the Davis stop to her office on Sherman Avenue, just a bit north of downtown proper. I was surprised to see she wasn't in an office building, but a rambling, turn-of-the-century brick house, half of its exterior covered with ivy. It was well kept up, with cream trim and green shutters. The walkway to the front door was lined with rose bushes. They looked very healthy and well-tended, blooming in shades of yellow, red, and orange.

Did she live here? Was I in the right place?

There were no mailboxes outside, nor was there any kind of intercom. I stood for a moment at the heavy green painted wooden front door, wondering if I should use the brass knocker to announce my arrival.

A voice startled me. It came out of the Ring doorbell that I'd yet to notice.

"Mr. Blake?"

I peered at the doorbell, noticing its light had morphed from green to white. I assumed I was being recorded. "Yes! Here for our six o'clock appointment."

There was a buzzing sound and the door's clock clicked. I reached out for the brass knob, turned it, and went inside, grateful for the blast of cool coming from the house's central air conditioning.

The foyer sported dark, polished hardwood floors and a big round oak table piled high with stacks of leather-bound books. A red and cream Persian rug gave the space a homey, yet elegant feel. A curving staircase with a mahogany banister led up to a second floor. I could see a stained-glass window on the landing. It depicted a cobalt blue sky and yellow lanterns that glowed with an almost electric power.

"I'm in here," a voice called out from my left.

I noticed a pocket door three-quarters of the way closed. I slid it back a little farther. And there she was.

Harriet McGill had appropriated the old living room as her office. The room was stunning, with more dark polished hardwood, more faded but elegant rugs, bookcases filled to overflowing with books and not knick-knacks, and floor-to-ceiling windows that looked out on a woodsy garden with wildflowers and pampas grass. I felt as though the L had transported me to an English manor house rather than a northern suburb of Evanston.

Harriet McGill herself sat in the dying sunlight, not at a big desk, as I'd expected, but on a lovely dark blue velvet couch. A glass-topped coffee table revealed a notebook, iPhone, and a pen lined up and at the ready. The woman was tiny and, in the right light, might pass for a child or an adolescent. Her feet, in sensible black Chuck Taylors, didn't reach the floor. She wore black jeans and a white button-down shirt, a size or two too big. Her hair, a mane of ash blonde with a streak of purple running through it on the left side, framed her face and curled just above her shoulders. Round red glasses magnified pale blue eyes.

I wondered if I was seeing a psychic or a private detective.

"Well, don't just stand there! Take a seat. The meter's running." She smiled.

I sat in a chair framed in stainless steel with dark gray cushions. It looked hard and uncomfortable and proved to be the exact opposite. I sunk into it, grateful to be off my feet.

We spoke a little in the kind of pleasantries people do upon meeting for the first time—the summer heat, the journey from the northside of Chicago to the northside of Evanston—but Harriet wasted no time, for which I was grateful.

"So, I took some notes from when we chatted on the phone, did a bit of digging in advance. I think I can help you."

These were words I longed to hear, and I said so.

She held up a hand. "Don't get too excited. I can

maybe find this Chris Sgro person. I probably won't be able to do much with your missing husband."

She stopped and peered at me over the top of her glasses. "Don't look defeated so early in the game! It's just that the police are already on it, as effective or ineffective as their efforts may be. And two, unless you have very deep pockets, searching for someone who may not want to be found can exhaust a lot of resources, both time and financial."

I nodded. I was disappointed, but she was simply saying what I'd expected to hear. I'd done my own search on our credit cards and bank account and, if Marc had left me, he wasn't leaving a trail behind.

I repeated the story my mother had told me while she was visiting and explained how it tied in with Jeb's disappearance all those years ago.

"And you say that this Jeb has contacted you again?"

"I said someone purporting to be him has contacted me."

"What's your take? Do you think it's him?"

"Come on. It's been decades. He can't have been abducted in 1986 only to resurface now. Why?"

She shrugged. "I'd like to say that was impossible. But I've seen enough in my years in this job to know *anything* is possible, likely even. If there's one thing I've learned is that the old saw is true: truth really is stranger than fiction. So, what's your gut tell you when you looked at this guy?"

"My gut? I honestly don't know. I mean, when I first encountered him, I supposed it could be him. For one thing, he had an amethyst pendant I gave him when we were boys. He has the same lanky build. The eye and hair color tracked."

I didn't mention the moles I'd just recently recalled in my dream. "He seems to know a lot about that time, more than someone could guess it or research from the scant coverage the story got when he vanished."

Yet I felt uncertain more and more as the days passed and Jeb did not re-enter my life. Now that I wanted him to—so I could at least examine his face for birthmarks—he seemed determined to stay away.

What if he never came back? Is that what I wanted?

"Look, if this Sgro person did take him back then, we may be able to find some significant stuff out. What I can do for you, since you mentioned you're concerned about money, is run a public records check on him. We'll start with the rather unusual name first and then, if nothing pans out, I can access a different database that captures known aliases of people."

"And you think that'll work?"

"I hope it will. I aim to please, Mr. Blake."

"Sam."

She smiled. "Harriet."

We chatted a bit more and I let her know how grateful I was for her help, for someone who seemed to care more than the police did. I stood and made for the door. "How long do you think it'll be before you might have something?"

"I should be able to pull some good info for you by tomorrow or the next day at the latest. Years ago, checking something like this out might have taken weeks." She tapped her laptop's cover. "Modern tech has changed all that."

"Okay." I reached for my wallet. "I can give you your

retainer now. You take Visa?"

She waved the offer off. "Much as I'd like to take your money now, let's see where we are when and if I get some useful stuff, okay? That way, you're not on the hook for more than I quoted and I'm not on the hook to refund you a portion if I don't find much."

She stood to walk me to the front door. "People assume, when they come here, I must make a fabulous living—big house in Evanston and all. But the truth is, I do this for two reasons. One, I'm a problem solver. This work exercises parts of my brain I enjoy using. And two, I like helping folks. Genuinely.

"This house and all its comforts? These didn't get here through me. That's all the work of my husband and his family. I won't bore you with details, but they own or manage a significant number of apartment buildings here in Evanston and on the northside of the city. If I were on my own, we'd be meeting in a McDonalds." She winked. "Give me a couple days. I'll call."

I left her and stepped out into the warm summer night. Dread and hoped mixed within me. What would she discover and would it lead me down another nightmare alley or into a wood even darker than the one Jeb entered all those years ago?

V

I was just getting ready to head out the door for my walk to the L train on Morse Avenue when my phone rang. I stopped, sat down on one of the back steps, and pulled the iPhone from my messenger bag.

Harriet McGill.

My heart rate sped up. Did she already have answers? Taking the call might make me late for work, not a good thing, especially because of all I'd missed lately, but I didn't care. There was no way in hell I could let this call go to voice mail. I pressed the green circle on the screen.

"Hello?" Even though I'd done nothing more strenuous than take a few steps out my back door, I imagined I'd sound to her as though I'd paused in the running of a marathon.

"Sam?"

"Yup. It's me."

"I hope this is a good time. You weren't sleeping, were you?"

"It's the greatest time in the world. Couldn't be better."

She chuckled. "Well, I did some digging and have some results for you. I'll email you a detailed report, so don't worry about taking notes."

I was glad of that. Taking notes would entail going back inside for pad and paper and in these times of tablets and touch screens. Who had those things handy anymore? *Not me, Harriet, not me. Now get to it...*

"I did manage to find your Mr. Sgro. Thank god for the alias database I subscribe to. It's not cheap, but in situations like this, it comes in very handy."

I wanted to scream. The suspense was, as they say, killing me. "And? What did you find?"

I could hear her mouse clicking in the background. That's how bated my breath was.

"Chris Sgro, at least the one we're looking for, wasn't anywhere to be found."

"Shit."

"Now wait a minute. He *was* to be found on the alias database and I think he's the man you're looking for. His real name is Keith Walker. He's also gone by John Soldano, Vito Weeda, and Mac Comparetto. He appears to like passing for Italian!" She snorted. "But that ethnicity is as fake as the names he chose. Keith Walker has been arrested several times."

"For what?" Even before she uttered even one crime he may have committed, I felt a chill that made me shiver, despite the morning's heat and humidity, which could be defined as the last gasp of summer.

"Abduction, statutory rape, kidnapping, sex trafficking, child porn, and attempted murder are the highlights, although there are more."

She recited the list like it was something simple—what to get at the grocery store, for example. But the power of the recitation turned my stomach, confirming the worst nightmares I'd had since 1986.

"Is he in prison?"

"That would make sense, wouldn't it? But here's the kicker: he's managed through the years to evade long-term confinement. Yes, he's been locked up, Joliet, Raiford down in Florida, and a couple other places, but through plea deals, overcrowding, and insufficient evidence, he's never stayed for long. From what I can determine, his longest confinement has been for a couple years and that was back in the 1990s."

So, if Jeb was abducted by this person and kept...and kept...and kept, he must have been free while the guy was incarcerated, right? Why wouldn't he have shown up on my doorstep back then? This information just made things curiouser and curiouser.

"Is he still alive?" *Please say no. Please say no.*

"Oh, yes." She paused. I swear to god I could hear the wheels turning, her debating whether she should reveal something else. "I'm going to tell you a thing and I want to advise you not to act on it. This is a dangerous man."

"Tell me." If she didn't, I wasn't sure my heart would ever start beating again.

"He's here. In the area. He lives on the South Side of Chicago, just a bit south of the Loop."

My mouth was suddenly dry.

"You won't contact him?"

"Are you nuts? Of course not," I said, knowing I was lying. "All this is in your email?"

"Yes, in greater detail. I could have withheld his current address, but hey, you're the client and you deserve everything I found." She paused for a minute. "I just sent it over to you. Take a look and let me know if you have any more questions. I also attached my invoice. Thankfully, what you owe is a good bit less than what I quoted. God bless the internet."

I stood to go back inside. I'd be missing work again, but I had to see where this guy was. He could be the key to everything. "Thank you so much, Harriet. I'll get your payment right out. Venmo okay?"

"Sure. Now remember, no contact, especially not in person."

"Of course. Um, is he on social media?"

"Not at all, so don't think of even checking that out."

"I wasn't." I lied again. I was suddenly impatient with her, wanting to get to my laptop and see more. I bid Harriet McGill a hasty goodbye and headed back into the condo.

The first thing I did was call work. Fortunately, my boss's phone went immediately to voicemail.

"Becky? So sorry, but I'm under the weather today. I think it's just that summer bug that's going around. I took a COVID test, and it's not that, so I hope to be back in the office tomorrow. I know I've been missing a good bit lately, but you know what I'm going through, so please be understanding." I hung up, not caring whether Becky Osborne was understanding or not.

I hurried back to the second bedroom, where there was a small desk set up with a MacBook Air that Marc and I shared for home use. I immediately signed into my Gmail. There was Harriet McGill's new message, in bold. My finger hovered over the keyboard for a moment. I was unsure if I wanted to open it. I knew I would, but I recognized this could be a life-changing moment. There was no guarantee that the truth would set me free or even improve my life in any way. I drew in a deep breath and clicked on the email to open it.

Before I even began reading, I knew this would send me down a road that I may regret traveling.

But the switch had been flipped, and I was like an addict whose drug of choice had been set in front of him. There was no turning back.

I skimmed the email and opened its attachment. McGill had outlined the basics and here were the details—arrest dates, times of incarceration, a long list of prior known addresses (none in St. Clair), and details about Walker's height and weight, date of birth (1958), and other personal details. But the one detail I both dreaded and was dying to see was there, near the bottom.

Keith Walker's last known address was on Roosevelt Road, just west to the Loop, heading out toward the western suburbs of Cicero and Berwyn.

I googled the address and then went to the Chicago Transit Authority's Trip Planner. I could take two L trains and a bus and be outside the address within a couple of hours.

Hey, I now had the day off and even though the prospect of questioning this person made me sick to my stomach, I knew I'd be unable to stop myself. I printed out the route from the CTA trip planner, folded it, and put it in the pocket of my jeans.

As I headed out the door, I refused to think of anything at all, and certainly not what might await me at the end of my multi-part public transportation journey.

VI

When people think of Chicago, they often think of world-class architecture, the ocean-like expanse of Lake Michigan at its eastern border, Millennium Park, the Loop, and Water Tower Place.

Many tourists never see the urban blight parts of the windy city. There's really no reason to, unless you're tracking a man who traffics in child abduction and god only knows what else.

The part of Roosevelt Road I stood on after the bus dropped me off was essentially charmless. Weed-choked vacant lots, litter, and a series of brick buildings, some red and some white, told a tale of urban decay and despair. Areas like these were where hope came to die. To the east, the skyscrapers of downtown rose up, majestic glass and steel castles, but they might as well have been in another world.

The air was choked with smog, hazy. The only smell was exhaust fumes.

There was a ministry/shelter that catered specifically to men across the street. Near the corner of Central Park Avenue (a misnomer for this poor neighborhood) was a white-brick, three-flat apartment building. It appeared to rise up out of cracked concrete and weeds.

This was where, according to Harriet McGill, Keith Walker, aka Chris Sgro, now resided.

Poor him. I mean, *literally*, poor him. The building looked like it could be swallowed up by the ground around it. There were several broken windows, a few more that were boarded over with cheap particleboard. Intact windows, grimy, sported sheets and blankets as draperies. The front door's long rectangular window was also boarded over and the wood had been gang-tagged. What vegetation there was near the three-steps leading up to the front door were yellow, dead.

Did anyone actually live here? If I were driving by, my first thought would be *crack house*. I'd remind myself I wouldn't want to be passing through the neighborhood after dark.

I took another gander at my surroundings. The streets were eerily empty. The only sound was the occasional passage of a car, truck, or bus. Further west, I spotted a sign that looked to be that of a convenience store and there were some signs of life in front of it. Three or four men milled about outside, wearing ribbed tank tops and baggy jeans.

I needed to get this over with as quickly as possible, as the area was giving me the creeps. This was a place where a middle-aged white man, well dressed and probably looking more than a little frightened, would make a tempting target for robbery or assault.

When I got to the front door, there were no buzzers. There had been an intercom at one time, but it had been ripped apart, wires exposed, rust eating up what was left of the metal interior.

"Now what?" I asked the empty street behind me. "Do I knock? Yell? Does anyone even live here?" For the last question, I got a quick answer, almost as though someone was listening. I detected a small movement behind the darkened glass of the bay window to my right, on the high-up first floor.

It must have been my lucky day because I heard movement from inside, a door opening and slamming shut, a cough, followed by shuffling footsteps.

The front door opened and an old Black woman peered out at me. She wore a housedress and worn slippers, and her gray hair formed a fuzzy nimbus around a wizened and freckled face. Black-framed glasses made her dark eyes appear larger behind the thick lenses. She was no more than four feet tall and probably weighed less than a hundred pounds. She'd shoved her hands into the pockets of her faded black-and-white checkered dress.

"What do you want?" She scowled at me, narrowing her eyes.

I could have responded like a smart ass and said something like, *well, hello to you too*, but, given the neighborhood and its obvious connection to crime and danger, I didn't blame her for being curt—or suspicious.

"I'm looking for a man, ma'am."

She cocked her head and smirked. "Then you want Halsted. That's where the men are!" She cackled. Her reference to the Boystown neighborhood was surprising, yet it put me slightly more at ease.

"Not in that way. I have an address here." I pulled out the paper and looked at it once more, verifying I was in the right place. "For a Keith Walker. Do you know him? Does he live here?"

"What are you, some kind of bill collector? Hit man?" She laughed and the chuckle ended in a spasm of coughs.

"No ma'am. Just an old friend."

"Liar. Walker had no friends. Least not from what I

seen."

I nodded. "So, he lives here? You do know him?"

"*Lived* here. If you're an old friend, didn't you know?"

"Know what?"

"He got himself killed. Last night." She shook her head, staring down at the gritty concrete at our feet for a moment. "Wasn't covered in the news. Most of the shit that happens around here doesn't qualify as news to the white people that run those stations and newspapers. But yeah, Mr. Walker was shot in the head a little after dark last night." She pointed to the convenience store a couple of blocks down. "Comin' out with some liquid refreshments. Drive by? Who knows? An ambulance took him away. I knew it wasn't good when they didn't use a siren or lights to head back toward downtown."

I was about to say something more, although I had no idea what, when she decided she'd imparted all she was going to and stepped back into the shadows, closing and locking the door behind her.

Shit. A dead end that was literally that.

In the distance, a CTA bus was heading my way.

What do I do now?

Chapter 9

Now—Marc

It was time. Time to do the right thing, time to tell the truth.

He'd worried Sam enough. He hated that he'd put him through such pain and anxiety, but he'd reached the end of his rope. Leaving as he had might have looked impulsive and unplanned, but the notion of walking away from his life had been with him for more years than he could remember.

He reminded himself that, although he was not as young as the anti-hero, Harry "Rabbit" Angstrom in his favorite novel, *Rabbit Run*, he was similarly disillusioned with love and life in general. In *Rabbit Run*, Harry leaves his pregnant wife on a whim, driving south to escape what he sees as a drab and colorless future stretched before him.

Marc reminded himself to go on Amazon and pick up a copy of the lauded Updike novel. He hadn't read it since he was an English major at Ohio State his freshman year. Although he could recall Angstrom's slipping the yolk of his dreary life, he couldn't remember much more of the plot, other than a baby drowning in a bathtub near the end.

He and Sam had gone through the motions for years,

perhaps even verging on decades now, devolving into little more than friends and roommates. The passion that had once been the glue that bound them had dried up, flaked off, and hadn't even been seen for so, so long.

The change happened so gradually he barely noticed it, much like the gray hairs appearing in his hair and beard, the lines around his eyes, the paunch he'd developed. But once he did notice it, there was no ignoring it. And the more prominent it became, the less he could turn away from the notion that his relationship with Sam was over. Love could wither and die on the vine. It wasn't anything new or unheard of.

It happened every day. It had happened to his Aunt Dee Dee and Uncle Jim after forty-some years of marriage. He didn't want to be like them, waiting until retirement until attempting to find his true happiness. He didn't want to look back at a life filled with regret.

In spite of everything, though, he loved Sam. But it was now a general kind of love, at best like a brother, at worst the love Jesus preached we should have for all fellow humans. It definitely wasn't romantic—not anymore.

He hated to hurt Sam.

He hated himself for behaving like a coward.

But if he hadn't walked out that hot summer day, he might never have left. All he could visualize for the future was days and nights of boredom, the same routines repeated endlessly, the mindless conversations with no or forgettable import, the steadily reduced desire for physical contact. He no longer even craved a hug or a kiss from Sam, let alone anything lustier or more sustained. In fact, the thought of touch repelled him. Even if he could see with his own eyes, Sam remained an attractive man, fit and handsome. But the spark had been snuffed out longer ago than Marc could recall. And, even though he couldn't help his feelings or lack thereof, he was guilty and felt awful, but he couldn't ignore the idea was a fact.

For a long period, he tried convincing himself that he should be grateful for what he had—a man who loved him, a nice home in a good neighborhood, a sweet little dog, and so much more. He knew men and women who dreamed of having a life like his, who would have taken what he already possessed in a heartbeat. After all, wasn't a long-standing marriage and a comfortable home the basis of the American dream?

Why, oh why, isn't this enough for me?

Why am I not satisfied?

Why do I feel as though I'm being slowly suffocated? Or worse, disappearing, bit by bit?

Questions like these—and the guilt that accompanied them—are what held him in place for so long.

There'd been no tipping point, not from what he could see, anyway. There was just that day not so long ago, with beef stew simmering and his beer bread cooling on the granite countertop, that something within him spoke very loudly. It told him it was time to get out. It was almost like an evacuation order—as though the idea of staying was impossible, out of the question, and he couldn't afford to waste time.

He'd taken only a few things—what would fit in his backpack and a small roller bag that fit comfortably in a plane's overhead compartment. He'd left behind so much—personal mementos like photos, books he'd loved, artwork he'd collected. Even his passport and birth certificate.

He figured he'd go back for them one day, once he had the courage and wherewithal to explain his feelings to Sam, explain them without causing him pain, a task he knew to be impossible.

But now, as he sat in the little motel room just a mile or two from the condo he'd shared with Sam, the Heart O' Chicago motel, at the corner of Ridge and Peterson, he thought he needed to, at the very least, put Sam out of his misery regarding his whereabouts.

So, after a long look out the window at the charmless view of the parking lot and surrounding city streets, at the overcast dingy-white sky, he sat at the table in the room and opened a spiral-bound pad of paper he'd bought at Walgreens, picked up a pen, and began to write.

The words flowed easily until he stopped because of movement on the bed, someone turning over, clearing his throat.

Marc turned to peer at the dark-haired man, shirt-less and hair tousled, on the bed. "I'm finally getting around to writing. I need to let him know I'm okay and—" His voice trailed off. He shrugged. "And to tell the truth—that I can no longer stand to be with him. It's awful." There was a catch in his throat. "I wish I didn't feel that way, but I can't help what's absolutely true—for me."

"I know. I know. As Neil Sedaka once sang, 'breaking up is hard to do,'" the man said and chuckled. He rolled away from Marc and pulled the sheet up to his ears.

Chapter 10

Now—Sam

Three weeks passed with no sign of Marc, with not a single word from him. If I wasn't so heart-broken, I might say it felt like he'd never existed.

Late summer morphed into autumn. The leaves began their show of colors, still stunningly beautiful despite having seen this display dozens of times throughout my life. I'd returned to work, but as a different employee than the one I'd once been—I did my job quietly, ate lunch alone, came in early and stayed late. My boss was happy, but the coworkers I used to hang out with, at lunchtime, in the breakroom discussing the latest episode of *Wednesday* on Netflix, or maybe grabbing a quick drink at the bar in the basement concourse of my building, were suddenly unsure of me. They knew I'd been through trauma—but not all the way through. Nothing was over, not really. I was pretty certain they understood why I'd become withdrawn, isolated, spurning their efforts to talk, to socialize.

I simply kept my head down and worked. My job performance had never been better.

I'd never been lonelier.

I'd never cared less.

Each day was a struggle—to make myself believe, to survive.

Yet every afternoon I walked home from the train filled with hope.

I'd imagine Marc waiting, a sheepish grin on his face, with some cockamamie story about where he'd been. There could be no reasonable explanation, I knew, but I'd be glad to have him back if only because I could stop dwelling on my greatest fear—that he was dead. I'd scrubbed away the bloody handprint on the door frame. The police had done all they were going to, which had never been much. The assumption was, and always would be, that Marc was yet another middle-aged man, bored with life and in middle-age crisis mode, who simply walked away from his life. It happened every day.

And who knows?

Maybe they're right.

No body has turned up.

No ransom note has surfaced.

There's no mysterious man in one of the many city hospitals with a head injury and amnesia.

No, I had to accept that either Marc had left me or that he had indeed been the victim of foul play and was, I don't know, buried in the deep woods of some forest preserve out in the suburbs. I had nightmares about shallow graves, a corpse tangled in low-hanging branches over the Chicago River, a pale body lying in a park, waiting for an eager dog to find it...

Today, I walked down Lunt Avenue, after disembarking from the Metra train (I'd started treating myself to the fancier commuter train, with its stop in my Rogers Park neighborhood, instead of riding the L). I had to cover more blocks to get to the L on Morse and the ride took longer, even factoring in my walk from the train station in the west Loop over to Michigan Avenue. But with all that had happened to me lately, all my fears and worries, I figured I deserved to treat myself a bit more kindly, even if it did cost more.

The smell of fall scented the air with a little decay. Some of the maple trees had started their scarlet transformation in earnest. Leaves littered the sidewalk. The sky, at dusk, spread out in a grayish lavender blanket.

I pondered over what I'd make for dinner or, more likely, what to order in, and what I might lose myself in this evening. Oblivion was my new best friend. Perhaps I'd draw a bath, light some candles, and bring a book to the tub. I was reading John Boyne's *All the Broken Places* and loved the story, disturbing as it was. I could, of course, simply be passive and forget my troubles with a good movie on Netflix or Hulu. The one thing I knew for sure was that I'd head to bed early, sleep poorly, yet wake with just enough energy to face another workday.

How long could I maintain this routine without going insane?

As I neared my building at the corner of Wolcott, I thought of the man who called himself Jeb. There had been no more contact, despite or maybe *because* I desperately wished for it. I saw him, or the man I thought to be him, many times, especially over the past few weeks. But it never was actually him, only a person that looked like him and often in only the most tangential of ways.

I'd gotten it into my head that this mysterious stranger knew about Marc's disappearance. He and he alone could unlock the secrets of my husband's whereabouts.

I needed only to see him again, so I could let him know of my despair, of my longing to know that Marc was okay, even if it didn't mean a reunion. He'd take pity on me and would tell me where he was, after prefacing the admission with the words, "I'm not supposed to say anything, but..."

I turned into the courtyard of my building and, as always, peered upward with optimism at our second-story window. Would I never lose hope that I'd see movement or a light turned on?

Maybe it was time to consider putting the place on the market. I could move somewhere that didn't contain the awful memories of this place. A fresh start could perhaps do wonders for my mental state. Even Mom thought so, and she'd told me more than once that I should return to St. Clair. My room was ready, and she was certain I could find a new job in Pittsburgh, which was only about an hour east.

"Hey Sam!" My neighbor Candace passed me on her way out with her dog, Asta, a long-haired dachshund, for their evening walk. Asta sniffed at my ankles, tail wagging. Seeing them reminded me that Vito would be awaiting my arrival with impatience. I looked forward to leashing him up and heading down to the lakefront.

In the lobby, with its rows of brass mailboxes, I paused to check my own. Inside, a couple of bills, one for car insurance, the other for gas, mingled with a Land's End catalog, and a flyer full of coupons I'd never use because I'd never take the time to look at them.

And then I stopped.

What I saw in the mail detritus nearly made my heart cease beating. My mouth went dry. A few beads of sweat popped out on my forehead.

In my assorted bills and junk mail was that rare bird, a hand-addressed envelope. Who received those these days?

But it wasn't so much the archaic snail mail communique that set off psychological alarms. It was the fact that I recognized the handwriting.

Marc's.

I was positive despite the lack of a return address, which, believe me, I searched for in vain.

I threw everything but his missive and the two bills in the lobby recycling bin and hurried upstairs.

Vito scratched at the door as I fumbled with my keys. He'd have to wait a few minutes more for his walk. There was no way I could ignore the envelope tucked under my arm.

Vito jumped on me as I entered and he followed me to the couch, whining his disappointment when I sat on the couch.

"Give me just a few, boy. I know you need to go and I got you, but this cannot wait." I could barely get the words out; I was so breathless as I ripped the hand-addressed envelope open.

Inside, a single sheet of lined paper from a steno pad, holes at the top that left paper litter on the hardwood floor. My eyes blurred peering down at Marc's handwriting, a mix of printing and cursive. I blinked. I took a couple deep breaths, and I began reading.

Dear Sam,

First, I'm sorry. And those words seem so meaningless,

so trite when I consider the magnitude of what I've done. Please read on and let me at least try to offer some explanation for what I know is odd behavior. I have no excuse, but maybe I can explain.

Before I get into my uncertain rhymes and reasons for my abrupt departure, I want you to know I'm okay. I'm sure I've worried you and, believe me, I know I could have handled this better, but sometimes life calls for immediate action and doesn't give us the luxury of careful planning.

At least these are the words I tell myself...

The truth is, and I suspect you know this already, our relationship, our marriage, were both dead in the water.

Dead in the water? I gasped. I had no idea. I didn't feel that way and I had no clue Marc did. Sure, things had gotten more routine as our years together accrued, but I always believed we had a foundation of love, family, and memories to rely on. And besides, didn't most couple experience some level of boredom and lack of excitement as their years together added up?

Vito whined beside me. I stood. This wasn't fair to the dog, who'd had his last trip outside when our walker, Tami, came by at noon for his afternoon break. "We're just going out front for a quick potty break," I told him. "We can do a longer walk later. I promise."

I got him harnessed and leashed, and then changed my mind. A long walk along the lakefront would do me as much, if not more, good, than it would him. The lake always calmed me. And being in view of it and around other, normal, folks might help alleviate the anxiety causing my heart to race and my skin to grow clammy with nervous sweat.

We went outside and I walked up and down the blocks, the drying leaves above me whispering, as Vito took care of business. We headed down to the waterfront, but it was no good. All the benefits I thought of being beside this literal great lake never happened. We turned around.

Back home, I set out his food bowl, filled with our homemade blend of chicken, rice, sweet potatoes, and green beans, and refreshed his water bowl.

And then I sat back down on the couch and took up the letter once more.

I'd let Marc continue with his fantasy that our love was 'dead in the water' a statement that I suspected would later rip my heart out even more than it already had. But right now, I was in too much shock to feel anything other than a kind of numb curiosity.

I took up his letter again.

When was the last time you touched me? When was the last time I touched you? When did we last felt like a real couple? I can't deny the truth—we were living separate lives and our passion for each other was snuffed out a long time ago. Who knows why? People change, find different paths. Life changes.

The end of a relationship doesn't always have to be someone's fault.

All I know is that I suddenly couldn't stand another minute of the life I was living with you. I know that sounds harsh and I want you to know that I do love you, but not as a husband, lover, or partner. I love you as the kind person and the dear friend you are. I know these words hurt, but you need to hear them so you'll hopefully at least have a bit of understanding for why I did what I did.

What I said above is key: I suddenly couldn't stand another minute of the life I was living. For me, the future looked bleak and, sadly, not worth living. I considered killing myself, which might surprise you.

I needed to get out, to start over, to live anew.

Before it was too late.

I turned the sheet over to continue reading. I barely noticed the tears on my face until they spotted the paper in my hand.

So, one day, without thinking about it, I packed a few things and just left. You can probably never forgive me for that action, but know this: I simply had to walk out. If I didn't do it that day, I might never have. I don't know why. Inertia? I do know that if I stayed one more minute, I was assuring myself a kind of death, either one that would take years or one that would come much more quickly.

I want to talk again, to see your face, to assure you this is certainly the old cliché about being more about me than you.

But for now, I need this time on my own. Understand, even if you now hate me. Or if you can't understand...hell, I don't know what to tell you to do.

I will be in touch.

I am okay.

Live your life. You can start over too. You might find that my walking out was the best thing that ever hap-

pened to you.
I hope the same will be true for me.
I'll be in touch soon.

Love,
Marc

I flung the letter to the floor, where Vito sniffed it, and then lifted his leg and pissed on it.

"Bless you," I whispered, and my tears turned to laughter that bordered on hysteria.

I sat there on the couch for the longest time. The night came along fully, stealing the light from the room, until I was that pathetic character sitting alone in the dark. Vito snored on the couch beside me. The evenness of his breathing lulled me. My head lolled to the back of the couch and I drifted off with my pup.

A dark wood. An opening in the trees.
Jeb moves into that opening, the shadows swallowing him up.
"Don't go back there!" I shout, but there's little volume to it despite the fact I feel I'm screaming.
But he hears me. He hears me!
He turns and, smiling, returns to me.

I woke to the sound of someone knocking on my door. I sat more upright, disoriented and wondering what decade I'm in, where I am. Vito stared at me with concerned brown eyes. I must have been yelling in my sleep.

"How did someone get in?" I wondered to the dog, to

no one in particular.

I stood and stretched. The knocking sounded again. I hurried to quiet it, thinking that even though I had no idea of the time, that it was late. I didn't want to disturb my neighbors.

I opened the door, unprepared for the psychological punch in the gut I was about to endure.

Jeb leaned against the door frame, eyeing me.

Chapter 11
1986—Jeb

I

Jeb hated to leave Sammy and Trudy alone to pack things up, but god almighty, did he have to pee! He was embarrassed over even the slightest indication that he had normal bodily functions, so for the last hour or so, he had held it, hoping the insistent urge would go away, to return when he was safely in the privacy of a bathroom with the door locked.

No such luck.

The need to relieve himself only increased and became stronger the more he tried to ignore it.

When he told Sammy, he got what he expected—a little ridicule and the attitude of, *dude, what the hell's with you? Just go.*

And now he wandered into the pitch darkness of the woods in front of him, hand outstretched to avoid running into a branch or worse, a tree bark, or even worse than that, a bear or a coyote. There'd been more than one sighting of both over the years.

Were there footsteps behind him? Sammy, trying to

get a peek? He'd laugh if it weren't for the darkness and the slight aura of fear surrounding him. He told himself he was being paranoid. The sounds were simply leaves in the trees, animals, and insects, all doing what they usually did.

As he finished up, shaking off for good measure, he noticed how his eyes had adjusted a bit. The moon tonight was bright, lending a silvery opalescence to the path he'd traveled. He'd come farther than he'd realized. As he glanced over his shoulder, he couldn't even see Sammy or, in fact, the opening to the woods.

His gut lurched. He hoped he wasn't lost. *Just turn around, put one foot in front of the other and go back the way you came. Simple. Easy. Don't panic.*

His last bit of self-advice was borne off on the wind, though, when he turned a little more and noticed someone standing not three feet away, watching.

Jeb gasped and froze.

The only sound for a few moments was the wind whispering through the leaves and the rhythmic chirp of crickets. A firefly danced in the night air, winking gold.

Jeb tried to swallow, but his mouth was dry.

The man leaning against a tree was older, maybe mid-thirties, early forties. It was hard to tell, what with the dark and his own limited perception around judging anyone's age, anyone who wasn't a kid, anyway. What made him look so creepy wasn't anything weird, though. He wore a Steelers black T-shirt and a pair of light-colored cargo shorts. Black high-top Converses. A black baseball cap. If Jeb had encountered him on the street in downtown St. Clair or, say, the grocery store, he wouldn't have even noticed the guy.

Before Jeb had a chance to ask him who he was, the man spoke.

"Sorry, Jeb. I didn't mean to startle you. I'm a friend of your dad's. Chris Sgro?" He smiled and Jeb relaxed, but only a little. This was still too weird. What was this guy doing hanging out in the woods, watching a kid take a piss? He wanted to simply turn and run, but that would be even weirder, right?

"So?" He'd never heard of a Chris Sgro and it wasn't like his dad had a ton of friends. Jeb turned back toward the path. He was pretty sure this was the way to Sammy and his mom. He took a step in what he hoped was the right direction.

"I came up here actually to find *you*."

"Really?" Now, that was odd. Jeb assumed anyone else coming up here would have passed them as they sat on their blanket in the grass. "How'd you get here? Didn't notice you go by, man."

Chris laughed. "Yeah, there's more than one way up here." He pointed in the opposite direction, away from where Jeb guessed Sammy and his mom were still waiting, probably getting a little worried. How long had it been?

"Okay." Jeb shifted his weight from one foot to the other. He noticed how silent the night had gone, as if the fireworks had left a vacuum in their wake in which no sound could be heard. "Listen, I need to get back to my friends." He didn't add, "I don't know what you want and I don't want to know."

"Wait, Jeb. Your dad sent me up here."

The statement did make Jeb pause. "Why? What's the matter?"

"It's your ma."

Jeb felt a bump in his blood pressure and heart rate. His parents weren't exactly Carol and Mike Brady. They liked, as Ma said, to feel good. "What happened? Is she okay?"

"I think she will be. But your dad wanted me to come get you, bring you to City Hospital."

Jeb shook his head. "Did she OD again?" He asked the question without emotion. It had happened before. And, as he'd thought many times before, a kid shouldn't have to worry about one or both of his parents overdosing.

"I'm afraid so. A little too much Peruvian marching powder, if you know what I mean."

Jeb did and wished fervently he did *not. Oh god, why can't you guys just be normal?*

"Come on. I think she'll be okay, but these things can go bad quick. We need to get to her." He pointed in the opposite direction again. "Quickest way down. C'mon."

Jeb peered into the shadows and could, indeed, see an opening and the beginning of a path. "I need to tell my friends." He turned back the way he'd come.

Chris Sgro grabbed his arm, but gently, and forced Jeb to meet his gaze. "There's no time, son. I lied. She isn't good. It's her heart. You need to come with me now. You can call your friends once we get to the hospital, explain what's happened."

"But they'll be worried." He imagined Sammy and Trudy waiting out there. But this was his mom. Could she die? His mom would never win any mother-of-the-year prize, but she was his. And she was the only one he had.

It was an impossible choice, but he felt the right way

was with this guy. He seemed normal. He seemed in control. He didn't seem to pose a threat.

Harmless, right?

Jeb knew it might not be the smartest choice, but he trusted him—at least in that moment. He sighed. "Okay."

Chris Sgro led him out of the woods. It was only a journey of a few feet. They were out of the woods in seconds. The path turned to the right and then dropped steeply downhill, a rock-strewn trail, where Jeb could see a van waiting at the bottom. Its color was hard to pinpoint in the dark. He assumed it was Sgro's.

Silently, Jeb followed the guy down to the van. Once they were there, Chris opened the passenger door. "Hop in and don't forget to buckle up."

Jeb, trusting of adults, did as he was told. All he could think about was his mother. This wasn't the first time he feared losing her. Flawed as she was, he still loved her with all his heart.

Instead of getting in the passenger side, Chris said, "I got to get something in the back. There's a loose oil can or some shit rolling around there and it's driving me nuts."

"Okay."

Jeb listened as he opened the rear doors. The eyes of an animal, glowing gold in the darkness, peered at him from the edge of the woods.

Before he knew what was happening, though, Sgro was behind him, reaching across his left shoulder to place a foul-smelling rag over his mouth and nose.

Before Jeb could even wonder what it was and why it smelled so awful, the world went black.

II

Jeb stirred a little. His mouth was dry and his head ached. His eyes burned. He closed them again, keeping still.

How much time had passed?

Why weren't they at the hospital?

He let out a small groan, one he imagined a sleeping person would make, and tried to shift a little to his side.

It was then he realized he was now in the back of the van, on his back. The cold, uneven metal surface hurt his back. The guy had bound his wrists and ankles. There was a cloth over his mouth, tied tightly behind his head. At least it smelled only of laundry detergent.

The road thrummed underneath him. There was no other sound, save for the van's engine and the hum of tires on pavement.

He'd been so easily trapped.

What's gonna happen next? Where is he taking me?

Chapter 12

Now—Sam

I

"What are you doing here?" I asked, stepping out into the corridor, mainly to prevent Vito, who was sniffing around my feet, from having any contact with the man.

"Can I come in?"

"Are you crazy? I mean, seriously, are you nuts?" This was all too much. I longed to get back to the life Marc said from which he needed to escape—mind-numbingly boring, routine, no surprises. It sounded like heaven.

My heart raced, though. I was afraid I might pass out. *Breathe, just breathe*. And I really tried.

It helped...a little.

Jeb said, "A lot of folks might say I am nuts." He smiled weakly. "But those same folks, every last one of 'em, will also tell you I'm as harmless as a pussycat."

"I have no reason to believe you." I shrugged. "Cats have claws and teeth."

"You're right. You don't have any reason to trust me." He fingered the amethyst pendant hanging at his collarbone. Was it a taunt? He retreated a couple of steps.

"Would you maybe consider allowing me the chance, small as you determine, to try to earn your trust?"

"Why should I do that?" I simply wanted to go back inside, turn both locks on the door, and go into my bedroom, where I'd hide under the covers, Vito's warm presence my only solace.

Yet I remained frozen in place. I said, "And don't tell me it's because you're Jeb. You're not." I shook my head. "For one, where are the moles you once had on your face?" I nodded. "I remembered."

Whoever this man was sucked in a breath of air and his mouth stayed open for a few seconds longer than what might be considered normal. He glanced down at the floor and then gave what appeared to be a sheepish grin. "As Joan Rivers once said, 'Can we talk?'"

I wasn't amused. No, I was anxious and sick to my stomach. "No. I don't think so. Not unless you're ready to give me some answers. Some *truthful* answers." I reached back to grasp the doorknob, indicating I'd had enough and was ready to go back in.

"Okay. Fair enough." He forced me to meet his gaze and when our eyes were locked, he said, "It's true. I'm not Jeb."

So, it was just as I thought. And not as I'd hoped. This is all a ruse. But what's the endgame? It wasn't money, that was for sure. Blood from a turnip and all that. "I knew it. I think I knew it from the first moment I laid eyes on you. There's something instinctive in us, something that allows us to recognize each other." I eyed him. "And I didn't recognize you. What's your game, man?"

He held up a placating hand. "Wait. No games. Hear me out. I'm not Jeb, it's true, and I apologize for pretending to be him. But what you don't know is that I knew Jeb. I knew him for a long time and, once upon a time, we had quite a bond. If you want to know, I can tell you what happened to him."

Oh my god. This is too much. I don't know what to say. Finally, a couple words came to me. "Tell me."

"Can we go someplace? Is there a café or something near?"

"Of course there is. Go on outside. Hang out in the courtyard. I'll be down in a minute."

I didn't wait for him to do as I asked. I scurried back inside, locked the door behind me, and went into my bedroom to change clothes. I slid into a pair of faded black jeans and a gray Keith Haring sweatshirt, red Hoka running shoes. I glanced at myself in the mirror over the dresser and asked, "What do you care?"

I debated for about a minute, thinking I could simply leave him outside and never see him again. But then who would answer all my questions?

I was about to hurry out to meet him, but not until I'd let poor Vito know that I'd be back soon and we'd have a nice, long walk, but only if he was a "very good boy." Vito looked at me as though he understood my words completely. And maybe he did.

He curled up on one side of the couch, head to toe, and closed his eyes.

And I rushed out the door.

At least this night, this strange meeting might bring some answers.

II

The Nervous Center was just a little south on Sheridan Road. I liked the café precisely because it was nothing like a Starbucks or a Peet's. A small storefront, it felt more like someone's living room. There were a few broken down couches, covered with bright quilts, scattered across the scuffed and dark hardwood floors. In front of each was a different thrift-store coffee table, piled with old magazines, board games, and decks of cards. A display case near the serving area held oddities—plastic shrunken heads, programs to plays downtown, the most recent of which was a road production of *Wicked* from the early oughts, a lightbulb, a rusty pair of pliers, a signed photograph of Tura Satana from Russ Meyer's classic, *Faster Pussycat, Kill, Kill.* The ephemera seemed to have no rhyme or reason, but it constantly changed and was never boring.

Jazz played—Miles Davis, Oscar Peterson, Duke Ellington, Ella Fitzgerald, and other icons. The music, soft, competed with the growl of the espresso machine and the coffee foamer.

Another glass case displayed home-made chocolate chip cookies, lemon bars, brownies, and an assortment of Danish.

I had no appetite.

We'd taken a table near the front window. Traffic flowed by, a bright-eyed endless train on Sheridan Road. I brought a mug of Earl Grey to the table and whatever-his-name-was had an Americano.

We sat in silence, sipping, although I suspect neither of us was thirsty or hungry.

At last, I repeated the words I'd used in my hallway. "Tell me."

He cocked his head. "Where do I start?"

"Your name would be a good place. But I don't want bullshit. I don't want some aka, you know."

"Fair enough." He leaned forward and, from his back pocket, withdrew a slim army-green leather wallet. He flipped it open to the part where there was a plastic shield over a driver's license and positioned it toward me.

I didn't touch it. I don't know why. But I did move closer so I could read the name and see the picture. The picture was him, no doubt about it. And the name? Hunter Graves. It sounded fake, like the hero or the villain of a horror novel. He was a year younger than I.

"I know, I know. It's my real name," he said. "If you need to see a passport—"

I cut him off by flicking the wallet back toward him. "That's okay, Hunter."

He picked up the wallet and put it back in his pocket. I wished I'd thought to verify the stats and, even more importantly, check his address. "Listen, there's a lot to this story. I can give you the CliffsNotes, but I think you deserve to know more. I mean, I know you loved Jebediah Kleber." He glanced my way, measuring my reaction to his use of Jeb's full name and his knowledge of my feelings about him. I won't say *my feelings back then* because I think, in my own way, I'd never stopped loving Jeb. That adolescent passion had frozen the night he vanished, almost as if it were preserved in ambergris.

Long ago, I'd looked up the meaning of Jeb's name, assuming it was of some hillbilly origin, but it was actually Hebrew and meant 'beloved friend.' *Yes*.

"How did you know that?"

"He told me. Many times. I heard all about you over the years we were together. See, we had little to do other than talk." He moved his head from side to side, stretching. "We were close—for a long time."

"So you were, what, a friend?" My heart edged up near my throat. The past tense and just the overall feeling told me Jeb, my Jeb, was more than likely no longer alive.

"We were close," Hunter repeated. The traffic whizzed by. He took a sip of his Americano. "I loved him too." The words, simple, came out with no real import or emotion and I wondered what kind of love, although I didn't ask. I wasn't sure I wanted to know.

Yet I couldn't stand the suspense. I wanted to know. And I didn't. But I blurted, "Where is he? Is he still alive?"

Hunter's eyes filling with tears, becoming shiny, told me my worst fears were about to be realized. His gaze, moving from my eyes to the laminate surface of our table, sealed the deal. I wasn't sure what I should feel. See, I'd kind of accepted Jeb was gone from our mortal realm—the realization had come a long time ago. But my dread was accompanied by its oft-undying companion, hope—that thing with feathers that could take flight with the slightest provocation.

"Do you really want to know?"

I slammed my hand on the table, causing the liquid in our cups to leap and scatter on the table. "Yes. Goddamn it." I sucked in a breath, feeling on the verge of tears myself. "Please."

Hunter reached across the table to cover my hand with his own. I snatched it away. "Tell me."

Hunter closed his eyes. He was regulating his breathing. Slowly in, slowly out. Finally, he met my stare with his own green eyes, so much like Jeb's. "You know already, but I can tell you need confirmation. Sometimes not knowing is easier—"

I cut him off again. "Just fuckin' tell me."

He reached into his back pocket once more and brought out his wallet. From the currency compartment, he extracted a small photograph, like the school portrait size one traded with friends, and slid it across the table toward me.

I stared at it for a moment before picking it up. I finally did. There was no doubt. This was my Jeb. In the photo, he looked to be about the same age I was now, maybe a few years younger—or older. It was hard to say. The portrait was small because it had been cut—jaggedly—with a pair of scissors. A mystery person had been snipped out the picture because there remained a disembodied hand on Jeb's shoulder.

He didn't look healthy. His skin was an ashy pallor, just a shade above white—a few purplish sores marred his once-handsome face even more. His eyes were rheumy, yellowish with broken blood vessels. His hair was dirty and even in this face portrait, I could see he was painfully thin. The bones in his face were prominent, the skin stretched over a skull.

I turned it face-down. The image broke my heart.

Hunter said softly, "That was taken last year sometime. He disappeared about a week after. Yes, sweetie, I think he went away, like a cat will hide, to die on his own."

"What was the matter with him?"

"Ah, do you really want me to say? I mean, I know you remember him fondly, or at least I believe you do. I don't want to tarnish your image."

I was ready to blurt out the same words that were becoming a litany, "Tell me," but quickly—and perhaps wisely—decided against it. All sorts of possibilities ran through my head, but the two most likely were he'd gotten AIDS or that he was a drug addict. Or both. The two often went hand in hand, especially if one was an IV drug user. These days, you don't hear much about people getting sick from AIDS. There were drug cocktails for it now—things like Truvada and Nevirapine—and they'd made the disease treatable, no longer a death sentence or often even a serious threat. I knew because I'd been positive myself since 1999. Thanks to taking care of myself and a daily regimen of wildly overpriced medications, I'd never been sick and had always tested undetectable. Yet I also knew people sometimes grew resistant or contracted a variation on the HIV virus that didn't respond well to treatment—or was resistant to it.

If he was a drug user, or addict, that would and wouldn't surprise me. His parents were both addicts. He'd grown up around it, seen the good and bad first-hand. Hell, with that mother of his, Jeb may have even come out of the womb addicted. Could he have the propensity for addiction in his genes?

So, he could just as well be pre-disposed toward drug use and abuse as he was against it.

But I wondered: *do I really want to know these things? Do I really want my last memories of my Jeb to be of disease, addiction, suffering? Or should I simply hold on the images I still retained—that of a handsome young teenage boy with his bright green eyes focused on a future of love, with me?*

"Are you *positive* he passed? I mean, do you, like, have an obituary or something you can point me toward?"

Jeb took a sip of his coffee. "I can't say." He stared down at the table. I did too, noticing someone had etched a heart on its surface. Inside the heart—EJ + BT.

"Can't or won't?"

"Both. Look, his death seems likely. We were in touch up until he vanished six months or so ago. He just wouldn't up and leave us, me, I mean. He cared. Or at least I thought he did. It sounds sick, but it's easier for me to think he died than that he just didn't want to be with us, er, I mean me, anymore."

The scenario sounded familiar. I had been more comfortable, I think, when I thought Marc might have been murdered. His letter was both a relief and a hard slap across the face, defeating my sense of self-worth. I was unlovable, I guess.

But just like that, hope returned. It wasn't like the sun coming out or anything. In fact, I looked at it as both a good thing and a bad thing—sunshine or storm clouds, depending on how I viewed things.

Knowing would have at least given me some relief. Not knowing at least gave me some relief.

There's a chance. He's out there, somewhere. Why are the two most significant men in my life doing their best to keep away? And why am I unable to let go?

I stared out the window for a long time. My tea had gone cold. The chatter in the café, a low roar punctuated by laughter, seemed unreal, the experiences of beings in a world other than my own.

"Are you okay?"

"No. Of course I'm not okay. Tell me how you knew Jeb."

Hunter stared into my eyes for the longest time. "I'm afraid you won't believe a word of what I say."

"Try me."

"You know that old adage?"

I replied, "Truth is stranger than fiction."

That made Hunter laugh and I had maybe warmed to him just a little. His laugh was, I don't know, innocent and vulnerable. He had a warm smile and the laughter, under other circumstances, would have been infectious. "You hit the nail on the head." Hunter turned to look at the round black-and-white clock on the wall. "What time does this place close?"

"Not sure. Probably ten, I'd guess." I glanced over at the door, where I could see the hours and days open in reverse, painted in bronze below the Nervous Center logo. "Eleven. They close at eleven."

Hunter nodded. "Buckle up, then, it's going to be a bumpy ride."

I tried to relax, but found it impossible to keep my spine from stiffening, to restrain my shoulders from edging up toward my jaw line.

"Go ahead," I said.

Chapter 13

1986—Hunter

I

"I think he might be coming awake." Hunter glanced over at Keith, who was driving the van. Keith's face was impassive, a sort of silvery-green from the moonlight filtering in through the dirty windshield. It reminded Hunter of the Wicked Witch of the West.

"Yeah?" Keith turned in his seat to peer toward the darkness at the back of the van. "Looks out to me. Do you know how much chloroform I gave him?"

Hunter shrugged. "As much as you gave me?"

"Don't be a smartass." He punched in the cigarette lighter and pulled a Marlboro Red from the pack, set it between his lips. When the lighter popped out, he lit the cigarette. The van's interior filled with an acrid burning stench. A wave of gray smoke rolled throughout the interior.

Hunter wrinkled his nose and lowered the window a crack.

"Put that back up."

"Oh, come on, we're in the middle of nowhere." They

were driving west on the Ohio Turnpike. They were about forty miles past Columbus. "On the turnpike, no one can hear you scream. Or smell your smoke."

"Funny," Keith said, the cigarette bouncing between his lips.

Hunter left the window open a bit and Keith didn't bother him about it anymore.

"The answer is yes."

"Yes, what?" Hunter asked.

"Yes, as a matter of fact, I gave him the same amount of chloroform I gave you back on that fateful day, or your lucky day." He turned to Hunter, grinning. "Depending on your perspective."

Hunter sunk back into the black vinyl captain's chair and closed his eyes. They were veering into a conversational territory he didn't want to enter. Maybe if he pretended to be asleep as he suspected the kid in the back, Jeb, was also doing, the talk would come to a standstill. Hunter had learned over the past few years that feigning sleep often delayed or rerouted devious plans.

He'd been with Keith Walker now for seven years, ever since he was nine years old. Walker, who'd called himself Chris Sgro, had dated his mom for a couple of weeks back in Hunter's hometown of Steubenville, Ohio. One winter night, when Hunter was fast asleep in his twin bed, burrowed down beneath flannel sheets and two quilts, dreaming of sugar-plum fairies, he'd woke to find Sgro standing over him.

"It's your mom."

Hunter had gotten to a sitting position immediately. The jolt of fear about his mama was like a stab of adrenaline straight to his heart.

"What's the matter? Is she okay? Should we call Dad?" Dad was over on the west side of town, in a studio apartment he'd rented when he and Mama had separated back around Halloween.

"No need to call him. Just get dressed and come with me." Sgro leaned against Hunter's bedroom wall, arms crossed over his flannel shirt, watching as Hunter pulled on jeans and a black sweatshirt. He grabbed his Adidas from under the bed and, after putting on socks, pulled them on.

Sgro eyed him the whole time, and it made his scalp prickle. It wasn't the first time he felt as though the man were regarding him a little *too* closely for comfort. Hunter wondered if the glimmer in Sgro's eyes was just his own imagination or if there was something that went deeper in the man's glance.

Downstairs, Mama lay on the couch. Her dress, a black velvet thing she liked to wear with the pearls Gram had given her on her wedding day, was bunched up beneath her. Heat rose to Hunter's face because part of her black lace panties were exposed. He looked away and asked, "What happened?"

"I can't wake her up. I think she mixed too many pain killers with vodka. I've told her before that stuff can be dangerous, especially together. I can help her out without getting the cops or doctors involved, which would be better for all concerned, but you gotta come with me."

Mama? She didn't drink much and she certainly hadn't used pain killers, at least as far as Hunter knew.

Hunter wished, back then, he'd at least insisted he stay

with his mom, who was in such bad shape. His heart ached and his nine-year-old mind immediately went to the worst-case scenario—she was dying. Her chest rising and falling was only a small reassurance.

"I just need to get out to the all-night Kroger's and get some stuff that'll help get her up. Now you go get in the van."

Hunter wanted to, but hadn't even asked why. He simply went out, climbed in the van, and sat in the passenger's seat. He even remembered to fasten his seat belt.

And then he fell for the same thing this kid, Jeb, did.

Chris said, "I got to get something out of the back. There's a loose pop bottle rolling around there and it's driving me *insane*."

"All right."

Chris disappeared toward the back of the van. The night pressed in. No lights shined in any of the neighbors' windows, which upped Hunter's anxiety even more. It wasn't a good place to be—all alone in the world with Chris Sgro.

The next thing Hunter knew, Sgro was behind him, reaching across his left shoulder to place a foul-smelling rag over his mouth and nose.

Before Hunter could even wonder what it was and why it smelled so foul, everything went dark.

That was seven years ago, or would be in December. Since then, he'd traveled the country with Walker, and done things his boy brain was too innocent and naïve to have even imagined. He'd been sold, traded, and photographed. He'd been used and abused by too many men to count (and some women, too—that part was even worse, because he'd always believed, based on his relationship with his mama, her friends, and her sisters, that women were kind and nurturing).

Through all the torture and the degradation, he'd remained numb—an unwilling victim, but a silent one. He seldom said a word, and that was okay with Walker.

Hunter was pliable and seemed willing, even though when the terrible things were happening, he wasn't really there. No, he retreated into memories—summers swimming at the lake where Aunt Amy had a little cottage, hiking the foothills of the Appalachians with his daddy and the beagle they used to have, Topper, shopping at the mall in Weirton, going on long, aimless drives through the countryside with Mama and Daddy, which always culminated in his getting a strawberry ice cream cone.

The stuff that was done to him seemed as though they'd happened to someone else. Even when it hurt, as it often did, Hunter learned to project himself out of the pain and the sickening closeness.

He found a way to rise above agony.

He'd become a shell—an empty boy with no thoughts, no spirit, no hope, dejected. Walker had stolen all the good and left an empty black hole in its place.

And Hunter had never found out if his mom was okay.

II

"Why didn't you fight him?" Sam asked, leaning forward over the café table. "Didn't you ever try to get away?"

"Early on, I did. A little. But he was older. He lied to me, so many lies. He told me my mama had died the night we left her on the couch. He said my daddy was so destitute over her passing that he blew his own head off. I was nine years old, man, nine. This guy, Walker, was bigger, stronger, older. Even though he hurt me time after time, I felt like he was all that I had, the only way I could survive. And he threatened me. If I ever did manage to get away from him, he'd track me down. And when he found me, it wouldn't be pretty. I didn't doubt him.

"You might not get it. You had someone you maybe took for granted, but who took care of you, who loved you, who made you the center of their world. I was a kid, not even a teenager yet, when all this shit went down. I couldn't get away. And, after a while, I just became numb, doing what I was told. I was an accomplice. And I wasn't even an unwilling one, just one who went through the motions because I didn't care anymore and because I never had a choice.

"That all changed, though, when I was sixteen, and he decided he needed another boy, a different one, younger. That's when he took Jeb."

Sam shook his head and leaned back in his seat. He lifted his cup, found it empty, and set it back, clattering in its saucer.

"I don't want to scare you or give you nightmares or anything like that, but you might want to know that Jeb wasn't his original target." He paused to draw in a deep breath. "You were."

Hunter watched as the blood literally drained from Sam's face. He went as white as the coffee cup in front of him.

Hunter shrugged. "It was a crime of opportunity. When Jeb went back into those woods to take a piss, it was too easy to resist, to wait."

"My god," Sam marveled. "You're telling the truth."

"Of course I am." Hunter reached across the table to take Sam's hand. This time, Sam didn't pull away. "Look, I know this has all been unreal for you. And what I'm telling you must be hard to take."

Just then, the barista stepped out from behind the counter. Hunter looked around. He hadn't even noticed the place had cleared out and the music had stopped.

The barista, a middle-aged guy in clear-framed glasses and a long green apron, neared their table. "Sorry guys, but I gotta close up. As the song says, 'you don't have to go home, but you can't stay here.'" He smiled and there was a kind of gentle reluctance in it. "You need to finish up."

Sam shook his head, as though waking from a dream. "What time is it?" he asked.

The barista said, "Going on eleven." He walked back to the counter and began cleaning up and putting away.

"How could that be?" Sam asked.

"Time just sort of slipped away."

"And we're not even having fun." Sam gave Hunter a half-hearted grin.

"You probably have work tomorrow, no?"

"I do, but I wanna know more. If I went home and went to bed now, I know I wouldn't sleep a wink, anyway." Sam stood and took both of their cups to the counter. When he came back, he said, "I have to get home to Vito, my dog. He needs to be walked. Would you maybe want to come with us? Tell me more?"

Hunter stood. "I'd like that." He followed Sam to the door. "I'd love to see Vito again."

Once they were outside, Hunter asked, "So, maybe you trust me now?"

"I wouldn't go that far. But I have so many questions."

"I'll tell you everything. I promise," Hunter said.

III

"Did you love him?" Sam asked.

They'd walked a long way south and were now at what the locals called the "gay beach" at Hollywood and Ardmore. The city called it Kathy Osterman beach, but no one ever referred to it as that.

"Why don't we sit? It looks like little Vito is getting pooped out," Hunter said. In the past few minutes, the dog had slowed his pace and exhibited a lot less interest in sniffing bushes and things like fire hydrants.

"Good idea." Sam sat on a bench overlooking the beach. The waves rolled in, their white caps made silver by the moonlight. "So, did you? Love him?"

"Is that important to you?" Hunter replied, watching as Vito curled at his feet. The dog continued to prove his trust in Hunter as they walked. Hunter had had the experience before; animals sensed he loved them and would never do them harm. "Is there a reason you want to know?"

"*I* loved him," Sam told Hunter. "I think back to when we were kids, it was a kind of puppy love. But his disappearance solidified it. If he hadn't been taken, it might have faded away. Who knows? I certainly can't say that I even knew Jeb all that well. He was my first crush, my first fantasy lover, the kid I fooled around with a little bit before I even really understood what sex was. So yeah, I'm curious to know if you loved him. And did he love you?"

Hunter stayed quiet for the longest time. The waves

rolled in and the sound of them, rhythmic, almost sooth-
ing, usurped even the sound of traffic flowing by behind them, where Hollywood curved into Lake Shore
Drive. The questions were loaded. They had so much
back story behind them that they would be here until
dawn's grayish light filtered over the water. He'd *still* be
talking as folks bicycled along the trail, on their way to
downtown jobs. Hell, he might still be talking into the
darkness of the next day. But for now, his best answer
was, "Yes. I loved Jeb. Very much. He was a lifeline. I
told you how I died inside when I was taken? When Jeb
joined me on our nightmare adventure, I had what I
thought was a friend. What was inside awakened a little
bit. And because we were forced into what I can only
describe as sexual slavery, we bonded very quickly, both
as friends and, not long after, as lovers."

"How about Jeb? Did *he* fight to get away?" Sam
reached down to scratch Vito behind the ears. "I know
you said you didn't. But what I don't get is that you two
were with this Walker sicko for not weeks, not months,
not even years, but decades. Why did you stay? Surely
there must have been opportunities to leave."

There were, Hunter thought, there surely were. But
there was the crux of the whole problem and he didn't
know how to explain it. He didn't know if he wanted
to clarify things for Sam because to do so would reveal
something he hadn't even yet hinted at—that Jeb Kleber
was a monster.

Hunter knew Sam clung to memory, to nostalgia, to
things like crushes and boyhood dreams of forever love.

To destroy that? Why? How? Could Hunter do it?

He and Jeb had reacted differently to their trauma, although the source of that agony stemmed from the same horrible experience. While Hunter became a kind of shell-shocked victim, suffering from what would nowadays be referred to as Post Traumatic Stress Disorder, Jeb followed a different path.

Hunter had been there to witness it.

The fact was it hadn't taken Jeb long at all to align with Walker. Jeb was just a kid, so it was difficult for Hunter to level blame at him, but the truth was, Jeb seemed to take to the life. He learned quickly to enjoy seeking out men. Hunter didn't want to believe it, but he'd seen the transformation with his own eyes. And it happened over the course of weeks, not years. It was Jeb who even introduced blackmail into their games, and that particular crime helped the three to survive, helped fuel—literally—their travels across the country.

In the end, Hunter decided he couldn't speak his truth, not yet. He'd unloaded so much on poor Sam that he didn't know what would happen if he told him Jeb had become, either through trauma or an inherent predisposition toward evil, a predator who was, in the end, no different from his captor.

And Hunter had remained by both of their sides. Walker, because he was terrified of the man. And Jeb, because, even though he became something Hunter would never be able to understand, Hunter loved him.

It was a sick, twisted love with no logical basis.

Hunter felt, suddenly, flooded with weariness. His eyes burned. His limbs felt like he'd run a marathon.

He'd said too much.

He hadn't said enough.

He dodged. "Can we talk more later? It must be well

past midnight. You have work in the morning and I have, er, things." Hunter desperately wanted to see Sam again and would do whatever it took to be near him once more.

"But—"

Hunter cut him off by holding up a hand, *stop*. "Soon. I'll tell you everything. Okay? Because you do need to know, Sam. You really need to know. I don't think you can ever understand, but at least you will have the whole story." Hunter turned and began walking away from Sam and his dog, heading west, toward the L train that would take him back to the southside and what passed for home. "Your life may depend on it."

Chapter 14

Now—Sam

I

I woke the next morning surprised that I'd so much as closed my eyes at all the night before. But I had. I had not only slept, but overslept. Brilliant sunlight flooded the bedroom, telling a tale of late morning as opposed to early. I rolled onto my side and plucked my phone off the nightstand. It was just after nine. *Damn. I'm gonna be so late for work. Again.*

Even though I'd missed far too much work lately with all this unexpected and unwelcome trauma, I decided I needed to call in sick just one more time. I wasn't certain I'd used up all the personal days I'd been allotted. I shrugged. The worst that would happen is I would lose my job or not be paid for the day. I'd survive.

I simply couldn't abide the thought of pretending—riding the train downtown, greeting coworkers and boss, going through the motions of a humdrum job that meant less and less as time and experience wore on. That world was for others, at least at the moment. Still, I hoped I wouldn't lose my job over this, but the idea of trying to act normal for eight hours or more was more than I could bear. All the pretense had been drained out of me.

I selected Becky Osbourne from among the contacts on my phone, pressed it, and waited to be connected. My prayer that I'd get voice mail was answered. I quickly explained that this time, it was not me but Vito who was ill. I said I'd managed to get an appointment for him at the vet's in the early afternoon. "I'm sure I'll be back tomorrow," I said, even though I wasn't sure at all.

Just as I was about to put the phone back down so I could get dressed and take care of the feeding and walking of Vito, the phone rang.

"Oh god no," I whimpered, thinking Becky was calling back, suspicious. She would say something like how much she regretted doing it, but she'd have to write me up. One more time and I'd give her no choice but to dismiss me. Or maybe it was wishful thinking believing she'd give me one more chance.

But it wasn't Becky.

My mother's name and face had appeared on my screen. *Odd. She never calls at this time of day on a weekday.* I answered, "Mom?"

"Sammy? Glad I caught you, hon. You're not at work, are you?"

"No. I called in sick today."

"I don't blame you, sweetheart. You must be out of your mind." She made a tsk sound. "So horrible."

I cocked my head. A chill coursed through me, making me shiver for a second. "Why?" I stood and slid in to pair of athletic shorts, a tank top, and flip-flops. Holding the phone away from my mouth, I patted my leg and whispered to Vito, "C'mon, boy." The dog hopped down from the bed.

"Oh, you haven't heard the news?"

"What news?" Dread arose, mainly in my gut. A wave of nausea weakened me. *What now? Don't I have enough to worry about?*

"Go check out the news. It's on TV, in the papers, online—even back here."

"Mom, just tell me." It seemed like my whole life had become a series of connections where I begged to be led out of the darkness.

"Okay," she said, voice strained and barely above a whisper. "I don't know anything for sure and neither does anybody else apparently, but a man's body was found in the wee hours of the morning at a place—let me look—in Chicago called Kathy Osterman Beach. Are you familiar with it? It looks like it's not too far from you."

I plopped back down on the bed and closed my eyes to shut out the irrationally bright sunlight. For several seconds, I couldn't speak. Words evaded me. The room swayed, making me wonder if an earthquake was happening.

Trudy cut in. "Look, Chicago's a big town. Lots of crime. It probably isn't Marc, but the description seemed to fit—the age, the general stats. I just thought you should know, so you could get in touch with the cops." She breathed hard, almost gasping, then added, "You know, just so they can rule Marc out."

The saliva in my mouth dried up. I struggled to get words out. "He wrote to me a while back, Mom. He's taking a break from us. It's sad, but it is what it is. I'm sure it isn't him."

"I know you're right, hon. But just check, okay? And then let me know."

"Did they say how this man was killed?" *Say he drowned, Mom. I can at least think it was an accident.*

"He was stabbed, left near the entrance to the men's room." Her voice broke a little, and I wondered why she was so certain this was Marc.

"Why do you think it's Marc?" I snapped. She was right about what she'd said about crime and the size of our metropolis. She paused and I used the time to put her on speaker and search for *body found Kathy Osterman Beach*. Two articles came up immediately from the *Tribune* and *The Sun Times*. Both described a body discovered by a runner near the beach in the early hours of the *morning*. The victim was a white male, approximately forty-five to fifty-five years old, five feet, ten inches tall and weighing one-hundred-and-eighty-five pounds.

It all fit.

I told myself that the description fit thousands of men, but my intuition begged to differ and caused the rat gnawing at my gut to bite harder.

"Oh, you'll think I'm crazy." Mom brought me back to the present.

"Mom, that ship has sailed."

She laughed, but it was uneasy, mirthless. "I had a dream last night. Woke up screaming."

I didn't want to hear about the dream. I didn't want to hear any more of this at all. I longed to start the day over, go to work as I was supposed to. Maybe that way, this phone call—and all it involved—wouldn't happen, wouldn't be true.

She told me about the dream, anyway. "Honey, I

dreamed Marc was dead. I didn't see the killing in the dream, but he was lying on the grass, eyes wide open and not moving. It's so weird. I was eating a red Popsicle as I stared at him."

A chill passed through me. Vito whined. "I got to go, Mom. I'll look into this more and see if there's anything we need to worry about."

I hung up. Vito pawed at my leg. I couldn't keep him in misery any longer. I gathered up my phone, put his camo harness on, and leashed him. We headed out.

Fall was coming. Although the day was sunny, there was an undercurrent of chill to it that made me shiver, thinking of what was around the corner. Would I be alone this winter? Could Marc have been the murdered man?

Even though I could tell myself—and I did—that it was unlikely that he was a crime victim, another part of me, the part some people called the gut or heart, or even intuition, told me it was him. My mother's dream was the truth. As we headed toward Clark Street, I remembered unwillingly the times Mom had had a glimpse into the future—when my fifth-grade teacher, Mrs. Mateer, was on maternity leave, Mom had dreamed her baby was stillborn. And it was. She'd also known our dog, Missy, would be hit by a car the day before it happened. Fortunately, Misty was with us a few more years, but with a limp and a terror of automobiles that never abated.

Dreams weren't reality, I told myself. Mom's past dreams were coincidences and nothing more. Yes, she was right about an unidentified man being found in the grass near our gay beach, but that doesn't mean it was Marc.

Vito and I walked for a long while, my stomach churning with dread. Finally, we reached another beach, the one at the end of Touhy Avenue, and I sat on a bench. Vito curled up at my feet, head up, sniffing. Since it was a weekday and cool, the beach was mostly empty. There was a woman with long dark hair flying a red and white striped kite, running across the sand. She looked as though she didn't have a care in the world.

I longed to be that woman.

I raised my phone and called the non-emergency number for the Chicago Police Department. I didn't want to—I dreaded what might be conveyed. But I told myself that it was even more likely I'd get news that would allow me to exit this state of suspense that threatened my sanity.

After going through multiple voice-mail-type prompts, being transferred twice, I finally got to talk to a live person.

"This is Detective Andrea Cawood. I understand you might have some information for me?" Her voice was gravelly, reminding me of Kathleen Turner.

"Uh, yes. I think so, but I'm not sure." I sounded like an idiot. And in a way, I hoped that impression might continue because it would mean I was totally off the mark about this murdered man.

"How about you give me your name before we go on?"

"Is that necessary?"

"Uh, not absolutely. Is there a reason you want to remain anonymous?" She paused and I could hear clicks as her fingers ran over a keyboard. "You do realize your number came up on Caller ID?"

I sighed. "Samuel Blake."

"And you're calling in reference to?"

"Marc Cornish. He's—"

The detective cut me off. "Did you say Cornish?"

"Yeah."

"Would this be the Marc Cornish whose last known address was on North Wolcott in Chicago?"

I nodded and then hurried to add, "Yes."

There was a long pause. I heard a cough in the background, garbled broadcast voices, and then, "Mr. Blake, are you available right now?"

I told her I'd be home in fifteen or twenty minutes.

I was about to ask if she needed my address, but she didn't need it because her next question—and it was no question, not really—was, "Could you come into the station on N. Clark, just north of Devon? Do you know where that is?"

"I do. I'll be there as soon as I can."

"Thanks. Just tell the officer at the front desk you're here to see me. I'll be expecting you within the half hour, okay?"

"Sure, no problem."

"And if you're not here within that time frame, I'll come find you."

I was surprised she'd say this, yet I imagined her smiling as she did.

II

By the time I got to the precinct, I was sick to my stomach. The nausea was so bad, it reminded me of last winter, when I'd gotten a horrible flu that had Marc contemplating calling an ambulance. From the chill and my own slick bodily dampness, I knew I probably looked as ill as I felt—whitish skin, slick, hair plastered to my head.

I also worried that all of this would make me look guilty.

I couldn't help it, though. I was now certain the murdered man was my husband. Despite the hurt I'd endured from his letter and his admission he no longer loved me, it didn't change my feelings toward him. I loved him deeply and always would—no matter what. He was my family as much as Trudy was. I'd never been open to allowing many people into that exalted circle known as family, whether that be defined by choice or by blood.

I expected to spend the rest of my life with him—sharing the good times and bad, growing old together. I thought of how we'd always planned to leave the cold and snow of Chicago winters behind when we retired. We'd move together to the sun and heat of the desert—Palm Springs.

When informed that I was here to see Detective Cawood, the uniformed officer on the front desk, a young guy with a blond buzzcut and piercing brown eyes, looked me up and down. He lifted the phone, spoke into it too softly for me to hear, and hung up.

He didn't smile. "She'll be right out. You can wait over there." He gestured toward the plastic seating near the front doors.

I barely had time to sit before Detective Andrea Cawood came through a pair of double doors behind the front desk. She was unusually tall, at least six feet, and her figure was one my mom once referred to as "womanly". Her hair was a bleached-blond halo with dark roots, cut short and framing her face. She wore a pair of navy polyester slacks, blue button-down, and a sport coat with a subtle gray and blue pattern. When it opened as she moved, I spotted a gun in a holster at her side, which made me even more nervous.

She isn't going to shoot you.

"Mr. Blake?" She called from across the room. I stood, feeling eyes on me, and followed her back. We went down a hallway and she led me to what she referred to as an interview room.

Inside, the room was pretty much like the ones I'd seen on TV in countless crime dramas. Linoleum floor, pale gray walls, a chrome-edged, Formica-topped table and two black metal folding chairs. The big picture window/mirror upped my anxiety level. Was there someone behind the glass, watching?

"I'm going to record this, okay?" She asked after we'd sat down. There was no fancy recorder, just her phone. I knew I wasn't really being asked for permission, so I nodded.

"Could you answer verbally, please?"

"Yes. I consent to being recorded." I looked up on the wall near the ceiling where a video camera was mounted. I knew my tone was dead.

Andrea Cawood sensed my nerves, I figured. She smiled and leaned closer. "I just want to ask you some questions, that's all. It's a simple process of elimination."

"Okay." I couldn't go on, though, not without knowing. "Was it him? Marc? He was the guy who was found, wasn't he?"

She licked her lips and drew her gaze away. Those simple movements told me everything. I steeled myself for the words I knew would follow. At the moment, though, I felt nothing but numb.

"I wish I had better news, Mr. Blake, but yes, the victim was your husband, Marc. They found a driver's license on the beach this morning with his name on it. His parents made a positive ID just an hour or so ago. I'm very sorry."

I wanted to feel more. I needed to break down in sobs—to shake, to scream. This awful nothingness inside was less tolerable than any histrionics I could imagine.

"I'll try to make this as brief as possible, but it'll help us with our investigation so much if we could get your recollections. The sooner you give them, the more reliable they'll be."

"Can I see him?" I blurted out.

"What do you mean? He's not here. He's at the morgue."

"I figured that." I shook my head. "You must have crime scene photos, right? They always take pictures. I don't think that's made up for TV."

"It's not," she replied. "But I'd advise against it. The images will be very disturbing. You won't want to remember him like that. He's gone, Mr. Blake."

"I understand that, but I just need to see for my-self. Does that make sense?" Without seeing him, even though all the evidence in the world pointed toward the contrary, my heart wouldn't be able to accept or even believe my Marc was gone without some form of visual proof.

She closed her eyes, whether in disgust at my morbid needs or because she pitied me, I wasn't sure. A black canvas bag rested on the floor at her feet. I hadn't paid much attention to it before, although she'd had it with her when she led me back to this room. She leaned over and rummaged around in it. She pulled out a gray folder. She held it close. "Now, are you sure?" She forced me to meet her gaze and, in her eyes, there was pity and a need to protect.

"To be honest, I'm not sure at all, Detective Cawood. But if I don't, I don't know if I can ever believe he's gone." I gasped a little at the word *gone* and forced myself to just breathe. I motioned with my hand. "Not really, not deep down. Does that make any sense?

"Please. Let me see."

She rifled through the photographs. I guessed she was looking for one that wasn't too gruesome. But with a murder, how could such a distinction exist?

At last, she slid one of the eight-by-tens toward me, face-down. "When you're ready."

I put my hand on the photo, but wasn't sure I could turn it over. Despite the stunned and shocked state I was in, my hands trembled above the back of the pho-tograph.

This was a moment from which I could never turn

back. Marc was dead, murdered, and the pain and terror of that happening was beyond my imagination. I let out a shaky breath and looked at the detective. "Could you turn it over for me?" My voice sounded weak and child-ish. I didn't care.

Detective Cawood stood and crossed the room, standing slightly behind me. She put one hand on my shoulder and, with the other, flipped the photo over.

The air in the room vanished. The noise outside the interrogation room—phones ringing and murmuring voices—ceased. For a moment, the whole world muted, as if its breath were bated. I looked away, toward the featureless cinderblock wall before me. Then I turned to peer over my shoulder at Detective Cawood.

"Are you okay? Shall I take it away?" She squeezed my shoulder with the gentleness of a mother.

"No." I shook my head to emphasize my refusal. I turned and forced myself to look.

There he was.

I gasped.

My husband. My love. His face was chalky, lips blue, eyes open, filmy, and staring at nothing. His lips were parted as though he had some final words to speak, but had never got the chance. His hair clung to his head. There was a very slight spray of blood droplets on his neck.

In my mind, disco music played—Sylvester singing "You Make Me Feel (Mighty Real)." Marc and I had danced to it on crowded dance floors up and down Halsted, the main street of Chicago's Boystown—at Roscoe's, at Hydrate, even at the more alternative and mixed-crowd Berlin.

I replaced the gruesome image before me with Marc's face on those dance floors. He always had eyes only for me when we danced. I'd once asked him why, when we were often surrounded by sweating hunks who'd shed their shirts to gyrate and grind their hips.

"It's like Sinead sings, honey. Nothing compares to you." I'd rolled my eyes at the comment, thinking it saccharine, but now I clung to it. Had he meant the words when he said them, or was he trying only to make me happy? Either way, the memory was bittersweet. I looked down at eyes that had once regarded me with passion, with love, with anger, with resignation, with annoyance, with joy, and now they looked back up at me from a crime-scene photograph with no life.

He was gone.

I bent my head low over the photo, shuddering, but not yet allowing myself to weep.

The world filtered back in, the sights, sounds and smells of the precinct—the laughter, the voices, the phones, the gray walls surrounding me, the odor of burned coffee over disinfectant.

I sat back up, straighter, squaring my shoulders.

"All right." I slid the photo back across the table to Cawood, who had resumed sitting in her chair. She took it quickly, slid it back into the folder, and shoved the folder back into her black bag. "What can I tell you, Detective?"

The warmth and concern she'd shown when she'd allowed me to look at the crime-scene photo all but vanished. She moved her phone a little closer to me on the table. "Why don't you start with telling me where you were last night?"

My stomach, already knotted *and* churning, if that was even possible, dropped. I had to suppress a gasp. *Where was I last night? I was at the very park where Marc was murdered, for Christ's sake. Can I tell her that?* I recalled all the detective and courtroom shows I'd watched on TV over the years and how the adage always went the spouse was responsible for most murders, or at least a family member. Evidence bore this out—it was much more non-fiction than a plot device, that much I knew for sure.

What could I do? Lie? Sure, and I might even get away with it. But even that much was doubtful. If I could manage to spin a tale giving myself an alibi, how would I frame it when Cawood would surely ask, "Do you have someone we can talk to to back that up?" Who would I say? Hunter? I had no way of contacting him. He hadn't even told me where he was living. And even if they could find him based on his name, *would* he back me up? Or would he simply tell the truth and say he'd left me alone near the beach *where Marc was stabbed to death*? If I didn't go down that road, what would I say? "I was home alone, watching television and then I went to bed." Who would alibi me for that story? Vito? I let out a short burst of laughter at that thought, a little giddy and bordering on hysteria.

"Something funny?"

"No." There was nothing funny in my world, not anymore. I wasn't certain there ever would be again. Should I ask for a lawyer? Should I simply clam up? Should I tell her I was leaving? After all, no one had said I was a suspect. I was free to leave at any time, right?

But how would that look?

Despair washed over me. All the weird occurrences of not just the past few months, but of my entire life, going back to the night Jeb disappeared after the Fourth of July fireworks, drowned me in anxiety and fear. I felt hopeless. I sighed. "I was home alone until I took my dog out for a walk."

"Where'd you go? About what time?"

Oh God, if get arrested now, so be it. What do I have to live for, anyway? My world has been ripped to shreds and then stomped on. My only worry—who would take care of my little Vito?

"I walked down to the lakefront and then south, to the gay beach."

Her eyebrows went up, but she said nothing.

I realized then her sitting there, hands in her lap, simply waiting, was a technique. *Keep quiet and let them talk.*

"Yes. Kathy Osterman Beach, as the sign says. Yes, where Marc was killed." Even though I knew it would do me no good, I added, "But I swear I didn't see him, and I certainly had nothing to do with what happened to him." I drew in a shaky breath, wondering if she'd say, 'That's what all the killers say.' The tears I'd suppressed earlier were close to falling. My voice broke a little on the words, "I loved him."

"What time was this?"

"Late. I wasn't paying much attention."

"Did you see anyone? Talk to somebody, maybe? I just want to place you, track your movements. Let me help you."

Help me what?

Do I tell her?

A voice inside, sensible, urged me to ask for counsel, to see if I could get out and away from her and her questions. I knew enough about police procedure from countless books and crime documentaries and podcasts to know that the police often weren't seeking the truth, but looking to close a case with any person who fit.

I fit.

I knew it.

Hopelessness caused me to answer, my voice coming out in a flat monotone. "Hunter. Hunter Graves."

"And who was he?"

It was time, I guess, to tell the whole truth and nothing but the truth.

God help me.

"Hunter Graves came to me last summer." And I went on, rolling out the story in bursts as I thought of various details, but moving back and forth in time, starting with Jeb's abduction. I even added what I'd learned from Hunter—how he and Jeb had been Keith Walker's prime fodder for human trafficking. I told her how the pair of them eventually split—a sort of yin and yang, where one was a victim and the other became a villain.

"I suppose they both dealt with the horror of what happened to them in their own ways."

I shuddered as something occurred to me—was Hunter wrong? Was Jeb still alive? Really, Hunter had only an assumption to go on. At least that was what he led me to believe.

And if Hunter was wrong and Jeb *was* still alive…

"Mr. Blake? Sam? Do you want to answer the question?" Detective Cawood stared at me. I felt as though I'd just swam up to the surface from a dream—or a nightmare.

"I'm sorry. What?"

"I asked if you could give me contact information for this—" She interrupted herself to peek at her notes. "This Hunter Graves."

"I only know his name. I don't know where he is." I did wonder if he was staying at the shithole on the south-side—Keith Walker's last known address. I'd already told her about my trip down there and now, I suggested it could be worth checking into. I took out my phone and scrolled through my email until I found the information the private detective I'd hired, Harriet McGill, had given me a few weeks ago. I opened her attachment and found the address and gave it to Cawood.

She jotted it down. "Thanks. We'll see if this leads anywhere."

We fell silent. I looked down at my phone and was stunned to see I'd already been here more than two hours.

Weariness washed over me. I thought of Vito, who was probably going nuts with his need to go outside. He rarely had accidents, but even if I were to leave and go home in a few minutes, it would still take me another couple of hours to get to him.

Marc was there, pressing at the edges of my consciousness and begging me to recognize, to see and absorb, his death. Grief waited for me. "Are we all done here, then?"

Detective Cawood glanced at her watch. "Mr. Blake, I'd really like to keep you here a little while longer. What I want to do is take a break and check out the things you told me—see if we can find any information on this Keith Walker, on Jeb Kleber, and on Hunter Graves. They might be linked to your husband's murder. They might not be. But I agree, the circumstances are very unusual and suspicious." She leaned forward. "I'll be upfront with you. You're now what we call a 'person of interest' and that means I need to make sure, before I can release you, that I don't need anything more from you."

"And what if you don't release me? What if the questions just keep coming?" I gulped. "And the suspicions? What then? Arrest me?"

She raised a not-so-placating hand toward me. "Let's not get ahead of ourselves here, okay? You're not a suspect. And if you really need to leave, then go. If you want an attorney, then by all means, call one."

"You think I need one?"

"I can't advise you on that."

"So, I can just go. I have a dog at home that needs me."

My last statement elicited a smile, which vanished as abruptly as it had come. "Do you have someone you can call who can check on your dog?"

I shook my head.

"As I said, you're free to go at any time. But I would appreciate your staying here. And, like I mentioned, I'd prefer a little time to check out some of the details of your story. Once I have those, we can make a better determination of what more I may or may not need from you. Okay?"

"I guess." Even though she said I had a choice, I didn't really feel like I did.

She stood. "It's been a long time. Are you hungry? I can get you a sandwich. Coffee? A Coke?"

"I'm okay."

She peered at me. "No, you're not. I'm going to have someone bring you some food. Eat it or not. But at least I've done my duty." She smiled. "In my other life, believe it or not, I'm a mom and half Italian. It's important to me that people eat."

"Okay."

She left me alone with far too many thoughts and worries, the biggest one being not would I get out of here today, but would something prevent me from leaving for a very, very long time?

And who would take care of Vito?

In spite of my refusal, I looked forward to that sandwich and drink. Not because I was hungry, but because eating and drinking would be something to do to stave off the tsunami of grief over Marc I knew was out there—and biding its time.

III

I began to wonder if Detective Cawood would ever return. And with good reason, she'd been gone now almost as long as she'd interviewed me. I was certain it was beginning to get dark outside. I felt like I'd entered some alternate universe.

She breezed into the room as though she'd been gone a mere few minutes, rather than a few hours. My back ached. My worry had peaked, and I was certain my freedom in this world was about to be severely curtailed. After all, why wouldn't she arrest me? I placed myself at the scene of the crime. That I had motive—a spurned love—could be effectively argued. I had no one, really, to come to my defense.

I eyed the handcuffs dangling from her waist and wondered how they'd feel around my wrists.

I wanted to ask why she was smiling, but I didn't dare. I was afraid the answer would be, "You have the right to remain silent..."

But she didn't read me my Miranda Rights off a card. No, she sat across from me, hands folded, with that idiotic grin on her face. If I didn't think it would go even worse for me, I would have slapped the expression right off her smug face.

But when she spoke, what she said shocked me to the core.

"So?" That was about all I could make myself say.

"I checked everything out as best I could. And it looks, Mr. Blake, as though everything you told me was the truth. Thank you for that."

"Okay." I nodded.

"But that's not the best part."

I slid down a bit in my seat. *Just get it over with.* "What's the best part?" I asked with absolutely no enthusiasm. I couldn't imagine what could be *best* about this whole situation. There may have been a *best* for her, but I was sure there wasn't one for me.

"Well, Mr. Blake, first off—you, sir, are free to go. You can take care of that dog of yours."

"Are you kidding?"

"I never kid." She frowned.

I believed her.

"What's second?" I was dying to know. What had she discovered during her time away that had caused her to come back with words of liberation for me?

"Jeb Kleber. That's what's second."

I cocked my head. The room spun a little. I felt dizzy and nauseated. *Isn't Jeb dead? Did they find him now?* "What do you mean?"

"It's weird. While I was tracking down the details of your story, someone came into the station. Without going into a lot of details, because I'm unable to at this point, it was Jeb Kleber. We've verified it."

"I thought he was dead."

"He's very much alive." She reached across the table and placed her hand over mine, squeezed a couple of times before letting it go. "He came into the station, the same station we're in right now, to confess."

I didn't know what to say. "He killed Marc." It wasn't a question. Somehow, I knew.

She was guarded. "Yes. That's what he's confessed to.

And right now, his story is credible. He knew details we hadn't released—details only the killer would know."

"Did he say why?" I took a sip of water. I was suddenly parched, as though my insides were drying out with each word the detective spoke.

She sighed and I could tell from the way her mouth was poised that she wanted to tell me more. But she caught herself. "That's all I can say for right now." She reached into her jacket pocket and brought out a card. "My card. You can call me in a few days and I can probably share more with you if the press doesn't get to it first."

I simply sat, slumped.

She smiled. "You can go. Do you need a ride?"

"I need a lot of things, Detective, but a ride isn't one of them." I stood. "I need to get home to my dog."

"Go. I've got things from here. And I will keep you posted."

As I was opening the door to exit, she called, "I'm sorry for all you've gone through, Mr. Blake. And I'm especially sorry for your loss. My condolences."

I rushed from the room, found the nearest men's room, plopped down in a stall and wept.

Marc was gone.

And nothing else mattered.

For some reason, as my tears abated an image arose—the beer bread Marc had made on the day he vanished. Something about that homely food—and the dinner we never shared—completely broke me.

Chapter 15

One Month Later—Sam

I

I held the memorial service for Marc at a small Unitarian church only a few blocks west of our condo on Morse Avenue. I'd waited a while because the authorities kept the body for the usual autopsy and to ensure all the possible evidence that could be collected had been. They still needed it, Detective Cawood explained, because even though there'd been an iron-clad confession, no one ever knew how or when things could change. Something that might have seemed inconsequential at one point might take on vast importance later on.

"Once the body is gone, there's no going back," she told me over the phone when she'd called to let me know I could proceed with funeral arrangements.

She'd been an unexpected source of solace through the trauma of losing Marc, the press's insistence on making a big story of it, and the grief I experienced at suddenly finding myself alone. She and I hadn't exactly become friends, but she seemed to care about me since the day I'd been interviewed. Although I didn't want to put words in her mouth or thoughts in her head, I suspected her affection and protectiveness stemmed from the fact that she knew, deep down, that I could never have murdered anyone, let alone Marc. She kept me posted on developments with the case and told me things she probably shouldn't have, like verifying the fact that it was only when Keith Walker had been shot coming out of a southside convenience store, that Hunter had been freed. Jeb, according to what she'd discovered, had managed to escape several months ago.

Marc had always wanted to be cremated, and I respected those wishes. The cremation had taken place last week and Marc's ashes now rested in a bronze urn on a podium at the front of the church, sheathed by a small piece of fabric—his mother's Hermes scarf the turquoise of a swimming pool. She'd always treasured it. Little did she know that her son had also always treasured it.

I was still in the process of figuring out what I should do with his remains (or cremains, as the funeral director had called them). I knew I could simply keep them and there was a comfort to that notion. They'd looked fine on the mantle at home, next to one of my favorite photographs of us, taken early on in our relationship when we'd driven all the way from Chicago to spend a week in August in Provincetown. A fellow gay tourist couple had snapped our picture as we walked down Commercial Street, hand in hand. We'd been young and carefree on that sweltering summer day, in tank tops and cut-offs, our smiles testimony to our insular passion. We'd become friends with the couple and the one, Robert I think his name was, sent us a print a few weeks after we'd come home.

And yet, I didn't like that idea. It seemed selfish. I knew, sadly, that Marc had yearned for freedom from our life together. I'd tried not to take his desire personally, but it was hard. But I thought a better way to deal with the ashes was to liberate them, to set Marc free on a gust of wind. I only needed to find the right place, a location from which he could soar...

Mom had been a source of comfort through these turbulent times. She'd bravely flown out to Chicago a second time, just so she could stay with me for an indefinite period, leaving her job behind.

I wasn't sure she'd ever go back to St. Clair. I was okay with that. I didn't care if she simply lived with me for the rest of her life. Nor did I worry about the potential for jokes about the middle-aged bachelor living with Mother. We'd always had a special bond, a sort of me-and-you-against-the-world kind of thing. Just as she had when I was a little boy, she hugged me late at night when I woke, screaming, from nightmares. She soothed me with her home cooking, her love of old television game shows, and the occasional game of hearts.

Now, as I stood at the back of the church, looking over the assembled crowd come to say goodbye to Marc, I was a little disheartened to see so few people there—a 'congregation' made up of Marc's boss, a couple co-workers, a guy from an LGBT book club Marc had belonged to a couple of years ago, and the dog walker we'd used. Of course, his mom and dad were there, a weeping indivisible unit in black, in the front row.

That was about it, except for one other person, who sat in the last pew, in a worn navy sweater and jeans, his head bowed. I squeezed his shoulder as I went by, heading for the front of the church. He clasped my hand for a moment, then let go.

I headed up front to sit next to Mom. She'd worn navy slacks and a white blouse. I don't know if it was the passage of time or the trauma of what her only son had gone through, but she looked smaller somehow, older. Her shoulders were hunched. She'd freed the gray in her hair and now, after several months, her shoulder-length bob was almost entirely white. It looked good on her, but she'd never again be the youthful mom people mistook for my sister.

She looked up at me as I approached and a sad smile deepened the creases around her eyes and mouth. Her dark eyes were damp and red-rimmed. I thought of a card she'd once given Marc years ago for his birthday and her note to him inside was about how he was just as much a son to her as I was.

These thoughts brought a lump to my throat—the impermanence of it all. Mom leaned over to hug me and I did my best to hold it all in. I was on the verge of all-out sobbing and I definitely didn't want to do that here. There would be time enough for more tears, yet another release, today and in the years to come. I knew I'd never fully get over this loss.

I disengaged myself from her when the music started. I'd created a playlist that played through the church's speaker system—Judy Collins singing the Beatles 'Golden Slumbers,' Sarah McLachlan's 'I Will Remember You,' Celine Dion's 'Because You Loved Me,' Whitney Houston with 'I Will Always Love You,' and Elton John's 'Candle in the Wind.' Sure, they were cliché and sentimental, but all of them contained lyrics that beautifully expressed the loss I felt, the hole left in my world by Marc's sudden and violent passing.

As Judy Collins's plaintive soprano rang out over the suddenly stilled church, I thought that it didn't matter Marc had left me for something else only he could understand. He'd been seduced by a conniving con man for one thing, a con man intent on killing to fulfill some crazy, blood-lust fueled need for revenge, even if it was horribly, horribly misplaced. For another, the fact that our marriage had withered on the vine wasn't something for which I could totally blame him. Every marriage needs two people to nurture it. And I knew now I'd failed him by being complacent, taking our many years together and the belief that there'd be many more for granted. Who knew? Maybe if the circumstances were more commonplace, Marc would have gotten his disenchantment out of the way with a bit of separation. Perhaps he would have returned to me more fully committed.

I'd never know.

And it didn't matter anymore, anyway. I loved him and I knew he loved me. That was solid and undoubtable.

The minister's brief eulogy went by as a mumbled noise. I couldn't concentrate. But I sat up straighter, as the minister, a lovely woman named Sandra, with short gray hair and severe black glasses that did nothing to lessen her light, her kindness, said, "And in closing, I'd like to read a poem by Christina Rossetti, chosen by Marc's husband, Sam."

I squeezed Mom's hand so hard she gasped, yet didn't pull away. She eyed me.

"This will be hard," I managed to say, my words coming out choked, barely above a whisper.

Sandra looked down at the podium and then raised her eyes to the small crowd.

"This is 'Remember Me.' Sam, I hope it gives you—and all here—comfort.

Remember me when I am gone away,
Gone far away into the silent land;
When you can no more hold me by the hand,
Nor I half turn to go, yet turning stay.

Remember me when no more day by day
You tell me of our future that you planned:
Only remember me; you understand
It will be late to counsel then or pray.

Yet if you should forget me for a while
And afterwards remember, do not grieve:

For if the darkness and corruption leave
A vestige of the thoughts that once I had,
Better by far you should forget and smile
Than that you should remember and be sad."

It was too much, the words too perfect. They seemed to have been written just for Marc and me.

A child again, I lay my head on my mother's breast and wept and wept until my eyes burned and my nose felt completely stopped up. I got lost in my pain, my mourning. I lifted my head only when the first notes of Vaughan Williams's lovely and poignant piece for solo violin, "The Lark Ascending" sounded.

I fought and managed to regain control of myself, for this was my cue to approach the altar. The minister handed me Marc's urn. I would lead the procession, carrying it out of the church. I'd thought I might say a few words, but I didn't have the strength. The poem had said it all for me, anyway.

As I walked down the space between the pews, head held high and with no more tears, I treasured the sympathetic and kind faces, all turned toward me. Just as I was nearing the door, I saw him.

My Marc, seated in the very last row. He wore his favorite sport coat, a subtle gray and blue plaid, white shirt, and bow tie. His gaze bore into my own. He mouthed the words, "It's okay. Everything is okay."

I blinked and he was gone. But I will always believe he was there that morning to say goodbye and maybe to reassure me of our singular love.

II

Another month passed. The trees lost their leaves and their branches, barren, reached toward the sky like skeletal fingers. The wind moving across the lake was now cold, even at midday. In Chicago, we put flannel sheets on our beds and battened down the hatches for the winter we knew was coming.

But today, today was different.

The temperature soared into the low seventies and the sun was butter yellow in a cloudless blue sky. Out the window, a person could be fooled observing that sky, thinking it was summer.

But the day inspired me. For too long, I'd wondered every night before falling asleep how I should take care of Marc's ashes. The sunshine and relative warmth of the late autumn day gave me an idea.

When Marc and I were first together, before we'd even dreamed that a legal marriage was a possibility for us, we'd cohabitated for the first time in a spacious and very old two-bedroom apartment on Fargo Avenue, about four blocks from the lake, but right next to the L tracks. We had to stop our phone conversations as trains went by so we could hear. But the apartment was huge, with crown moldings, hardwood floors, fireplace, built-in cabinets, butler's pantry, an original claw-foot tub, and huge windows that lured shafts of sunlight in. It had a ton of charm. It also had mice, ancient appliances, noisy neighbors, and the surrounding area could be a little dicey at night.

But during the day, especially during warm summer ones, Fargo Avenue Beach was but a few blocks away, a ten-minute walk. We accessed the beach by a set of broad concrete stairs. The sand was always fine, the water pristine, and there was a small island comprised of boulders within easy swimming distance.

Marc and I spent countless carefree days on that beach. We would anchor an old sheet down by folding the corners into the sand. We'd sprawl out on it, playing music on the relic of an old boombox I'd held on to since the 1990s. The air was scented with coconut oil and we'd spend entire days, lost in conversation, drinking Cosmopolitans from a thermos, and sharing pimento cheese and saltines. One of the reasons we adored this place so much was because it was always relatively empty, being about as far north in the city as one could get.

Somedays, it felt like our own private beach.

Marc, I knew, would love the idea of this beach as his final resting place.

The day was perfect for the task. I thought of waiting for Mom to get back from St. Clair, where she'd gone for a couple of weeks to settle her affairs before moving back here permanently. She'd be disappointed because she loved Marc about as much as I did. I hoped she'd understand.

I did invite one person to join me. I hadn't intended to, but when Hunter texted me that morning, I decided on a whim it would be nice to have him with me. His part in this story was undeniable, even if it did have gothic and gruesome overtones. I'd learned, though, that Hunter was as much of a victim as I was and as Marc was. He was no villain and I'd grown to care about him. Call me weird. You won't be the first.

Besides, there remained one burning question I needed to ask him. The answer to the riddle was vital for me to decide if I wanted to continue having him in my life in a way I'd yet to define, or if I should do the mentally healthy thing of cutting him loose.

I seldom did the mentally healthy thing, which Mom will attest to.

I went to the mantel and opened the urn. Inside was a plastic bag of ashes, although calling them ashes seemed wrong. I'd held a handful and what remained of Marc (after most parts of him were vaporized by the furnace) was more akin to sand, but grayish white sand. They felt rough to the touch and small bone particles were visible and a little larger than the 'sand' of him.

I'd been squeamish at first, but the remains had become a comfort to me. Looking at them and holding them was a way for me to be in physical contact once more with Marc. I decided I would withhold about a teaspoon of them to, I don't know, put in a pendant or maybe a small piece of glass art.

No matter what, going forward I wanted him with me in at least a small way. He was an undeniable and important part of my personal history. Our years together wouldn't evaporate, even over something as final and omnipotent as death.

Death never erases our bonds with one another; those live on in hearts primed with memories and love.

I placed Marc's remains into a silver Nordstrom shopping bag and went downstairs to wait for Hunter. He'd arrive any moment.

III

Hunter and I sat on the beach for a long time before I wanted to do anything with the remains. We'd spread out a couple of beach towels and lounged in the sand, legs outstretched, simply watching the ebb and flow of the waves and how the sunlight shimmered on the slate gray surface of the water.

At the south end of the beach, a woman with two kids, boy and girl, tossed a beach ball back and forth. We watched them as they played. Being kids, they'd rolled up their jeans and dared each other to wade into the icy water. They would scream when they did and dash back to the safety of their mother once the water's icy embrace touched them.

A young guy with longish honey-colored hair, cargo shorts, a Green Day T-shirt, and Vans, frolicked with a German Shepherd. He'd toss a Frisbee into the water, which the dog would catch expertly in its mouth even as the water splashed up all around him.

Distractions.

I knew what I was doing.

Avoidance.

I wasn't sure, now that Hunter was by my side, a warm and comfortable presence indeed—that I wanted to share this very private moment with him, especially given his connection, however innocent, with Marc's death.

Why bring him along, then?

I think it was because I hadn't really examined my

motive, not with this grief hanging over me. Not with the loneliness pressing in, especially with Mom back in St. Clair. I wanted *someone* with me, and he seemed like the only person in the world who would truly understand and empathize with what I was going through. Other friends and acquaintances had suddenly made themselves unavailable, barely responding to the usual forms of contact—social media posts and texts. I didn't blame them. My situation had become bizarre. Not knowing how to respond was understandable. Perhaps one day, they'd glide back into my life, once recent events had paled into the background.

Hunter had been very supportive, though, taking my calls and texts at all hours and trying, in his own way, to let me know I was seen and cared for. Given his history with Jeb and Keith Walker, this was no small thing.

But I think the real reason I wanted him here was to ask the question that had been needling me for months now. I'd never had the courage to ask. I don't know why. Maybe I feared embarrassing him when he'd actually bent over backwards to demonstrate to me nothing but kindness. Or maybe it was me who was fearful—of what his answer might be.

The man with the dog abruptly left and we were essentially alone at the north end of the beach. There was a soft breeze off the water. A few puffy clouds had rolled in, adding drama to the sky and big shadows to the beach.

"I need to ask you something." I stared out at the water, almost afraid to look at him. I dug in the sand with my hand and let it flow through my fingers. I stopped when I realized that the sand reminded me of Marc's remains.

Hunter touched my arm. "What is it? You know you can ask me anything."

Can I?

"Well, I've wondered why you came to me as Jeb. Why didn't you just come as yourself? Why did you feel the need to pretend?"

He said nothing for several minutes, and then, "Look at me."

I turned my head and Hunter waited until our gazes met. "Don't be creeped out. At least not more than you already are." He smiled. "But I'd been watching you for a while, actually, since the previous winter when Keith, Jeb, and I moved to Chicago from LA, where we'd been before.

"Jeb had told me all about you and that he'd looked you up and knew where you were. He said nothing, back then, about wanting to hurt you or get even or whatever was going on with him. No, he spoke with great fondness about you, at least at first.

"If it means something, he told me the whole story of when you were kids and how you fooled around and had this whole puppy love thing going on.

"It made me curious about you. See, I was taken so young, I never had anybody in my life. I never knew what falling in love even meant.

"And then I watched you come and go with Marc. I could see how comfortable you were with each other. There was an ease in the way you looked at the other, in your casual touches.

"Now know that I didn't watch you a lot. I'd come up and stroll around the neighborhood, go down to the lakefront. I saw you guys maybe a total of three times, if that."

"Okay, okay. But you're not answering the question. Why did you pretend to be Jeb?"

Hunter shut down a little. I could tell he was thinking. "It was the story Jeb told me. The two of you swimming together in the river. The stolen kisses." Hunter reached down and grasped the amethyst pendant still hanging there. "He gave me this. He said you'd given it to him, to protect him. No one, and he emphasized *no one*, had ever tried to protect him before, especially not his parents."

"Why then, would he give it to you?"

"Because things were starting to fall apart by that time. I could tell he was jealous that you had someone. Totally irrational, I know. You'd been kids when you last saw each other. But I knew, from his reactions when I'd report on how you were doing and that I'd seen you with Marc, that he saw the love you had for your own husband, *thirty-some years later*, as a betrayal.

"I think that's when he started fantasizing about hurting you—or worse. It was no coincidence that it was also when he started getting more heavily into drugs. He was always into them and booze, always, but things started to take a turn for the worse when some dude introduced him to meth. He got hooked almost instantly. Walker encouraged it too. It made Jeb more 'pliable,' he said." Hunter shook his head, remembering.

"More than ever, I wanted out. To be free was all I could dream of. When Keith died, setting us both free, I wanted to meet you, to get to you before Jeb could. And in some crazy way, I thought if you believed I was Jeb, you wouldn't believe the real Jeb when he one day would show up."

He eyed me and I could read the terror in his face.

"I also thought you might come to see me as a person you could love, as you once loved Jeb. He and I looked similar enough that I thought I could pass." He stretched out a bit, raising his face to the sun for a moment. "Crazy, right?" He made a little circling motion at the side of his head, the international symbol for absolutely nuts.

"I wanted that puppy love. I wanted *you*. And I thought I stood a better chance if you thought I was your long-lost love."

The words caught me up short. Even though I'd imagined this as the reason for his masquerading as Jeb, I couldn't quite get my mind around his rationale. I felt confused and lost. These were not the feelings I wanted to bring to this ceremonial farewell.

"Hunter," I said after a long pause and him appearing distressed and worried. "I need you to go."

"Oh no. I was afraid this would happen."

"No, no. Please don't worry. I don't mean go *forever*. But I need to process." I leaned forward to touch the silver bag containing Marc's ashes. "And I really need to be alone."

"Are you sure?"

"Oh yes."

Awkwardly, Hunter rose to his feet. He appeared hurt, cast out. But I couldn't help that. At least not right now.

We didn't say anything more. I watched him leave the beach without looking back, and knew he was afraid I was casting him out for good.

But I didn't know what I wanted. I had too much to think about.

And Marc needed a proper goodbye, just between the two of us.

IV

I stayed on the beach until the sky started to darken and the sun, behind me, set behind the mix of brick and mortar that was the city.

People had come and gone as I sat there, fingers in the cool sand—a gay couple obviously early on in their relationship, an older woman with frizzy salt and pepper hair and a copy of Douglas Stuart's *Young Mungo* open on her lap, a few other people with dogs, taking the opportunity to break the law and let them run free along the shoreline, and an old man with a metal detector and headphones, searching, I guess for change and lost jewelry.

But just as the sky was getting murky, a kind of grayish lavender in color, I at last had the beach to myself.

The moment had come.

I rose, shaky as a newborn foal taking its first step. I removed the plastic bag with the ashes from the Nordstrom shopping bag. It felt both heavy and light at the same time. I'd guess it weighed maybe a little more than a couple of pounds. So, the actual heft of the thing was what felt light. What felt heavy was that this was all that was left of my man.

Scenes of our life together ran through my mind—the passion at the start, the nesting as we searched for our forever home in our favorite Chicago neighborhood, Rogers Park, the trips to places near and far, like Saugatuck, Michigan across the lake, where there was a gay campground called Camp It to far away, a once-in-a-lifetime trip to Rome, Milan, and Florence for Marc's 40th. My happiest memories were simple, though—picking up Vito from the animal shelter when he was a puppy, nights on the couch with a Giordano's pizza and a couple of beers on the coffee table before us as we binged something like *The Marvelous Mrs. Maisel* on Amazon Prime or *Ted Lasso* on Apple TV, grocery shopping, trips up to Lake Geneva or Door County to take in autumn foliage. Even something as simple as an L train ride downtown to see a play were cemented into my head, memories I'd now treasure even more than I'd ever dreamed.

I moved with the plastic bag toward the water. I glanced behind me to make sure I was still alone. I wasn't sure what I was about to do was even legal, so I wanted to take care. I also simply wanted to be alone with Marc.

I set the bag down on the sand and squatted to open it. I dug into the ashes, grasping as big of a handful as my fingers would allow.

I neared the water's edge, just close enough to avoid getting my feet wet. The water had gone still as the wind suddenly disappeared. I heard traffic behind me on Sheridan Road, a snatch of conversation and laughter coming from an open apartment window, and a bit of music, maybe from a car, Adele singing "Hello."

"I will never stop missing you. I will never stop loving you. You are a jagged little piece of my heart, just as painful, but also just as life-giving. You run through my veins and my dreams."

I thought a bit longer, but the words were enough. If Marc could somehow listen, I hoped he'd understand that he'd been, for many, many years, the most important person in my life. He was my dawn, my dusk, and my midday.

I flung the handful of ashes outward, over the mirror-like surface of the water, watching it rise just a bit and then tumble into the water, sinking.

I reached in for another handful and repeated the process. Again. And again, until all that was left was maybe a quarter of a cup. I'd keep half of that for myself. I'd give the other half to Marc's mom and dad.

I gathered up my things.

Darkness had claimed the beach and I needed to get home.

Chapter 16

Now—Sam

I

It had been a long and exhausting trip.

Since I sold my Prius last winter when it was more of a hassle in the city than it was worth, I took public transportation everywhere. Most of the time, it was quick and convenient, and I barely missed the car Marc and I once shared. I certainly didn't miss traffic jams and searching for an hour for street parking.

This trip—from Rogers Park to the Cook County Jail on the southside—was testing my nerves and my patience. It involved a Red Line and a Green Line L train and a couple of different buses.

Even though it was April, it was cold. Dirty snow defined the landscape and, above it, a dingy grayish sky filtered the sun begrudgingly, lending a washed-out feeble light to the day. The temperature hovered just above freezing. The wind off of the lake contributed to the wind chill.

My current bus had no heat, at least not the kind provided by its own works. I suppose I should have been grateful that the bus was crowded with people, which made for a kind of body heat blanket. Never mind the smell!

I had delayed making this visit for too long. Sure, I had seen Jeb during the trial last year and our eyes had even met a couple of times when he was being led into the courtroom, but I had not had any contact with him since that terrible late summer day when I'd been interrogated for hours and hours and was only freed because Jeb had, in some last-minute drama only he could understand and orchestrate, had come in to the very same police station where I was being questioned and confessed to killing my husband and, really, the love of my life. He may as well have confessed to snuffing out all the happiness and hope I had.

I hadn't wanted to talk to him.

I hadn't needed to talk to him.

I wanted, truly, to banish him from my life, my memories, and my nightmares.

It took me several months to realize that what I wanted was impossible. Short of undergoing some kind of lobotomy, my experiences with Jeb, both as a youth and as a middle-aged man, were now a permanent part of my history, whether I wanted them as part of that record or not.

Jeb was an unwelcome visitor, though, on an almost daily basis. He appeared in dreams, in memories, and in my confounding desire to know how he could have changed so much over the years from the young man I thought I'd known.

II

We faced one another across a table in a room as gray as the wintry sky outside the prison. Jeb was in an orange jumpsuit, dark hair shorn down to his scalp, with multiple crude tattoos peeking out from just about anywhere the orange didn't cover. His wrists were cuffed and, beneath our scarred table, his ankles were bound by a heavy chain.

His green eyes were the only thing I was at ease focusing on. It was because they were about the only aspect of him I could recall from those glorious days when I was thirteen years old and madly in love with this boy.

I had to wonder—had he already been evil when we knew each other back then? Was he only hiding it? Or, more likely, had the trauma of what had been done to him transformed him into a monster?

I supposed I could ask him, but who knows what kind of answer he'd have for me? Who knows if even he was aware of the why of his own broken psyche?

He regarded me with a blank expression, staring across the table and the low divider separating us. His expression lacked guile, expectation, recognition, or really much emotion at all. He didn't say a word, not even hello, so I guessed he was waiting for my cue.

"Thanks for seeing me. You certainly didn't have to put me on your visitor list."

He nodded, expression remaining neutral. I began to wonder if coming here had been a mistake. What good would it do me?

"I was curious." His voice was deep, a rich baritone, and nothing like the breaking adolescent voice I remembered even now. It was the voice of a man I didn't know.

I fell silent. Have you ever been in a situation where stringing together a few words became an almost Herculean task? Overwhelmed with pain, regret, and a kind of morbid curiosity, I struggled with how to conduct this conversation.

What do you really want to know? Ask that.

So, I did.

"Why? I came to court every day to try and figure it out, but your lawyer never allowed you to take the stand. And frankly, no one cared much about the why. But I care and maybe it'll help me with closure if I know."

"You want me to help you?" His face went from neutral to a sneer. I felt his view of me was akin to someone looking at a cockroach, and I shrank back in my seat a little. This was a moment I recognized for what it was—if I had any doubt that the Jeb I knew all those years ago in St. Clair was gone for good, then that doubt was now erased.

"It's up to you, Jeb." I felt odd even using his first name, since he was essentially now a stranger to me, although life would forever bind us up in ways that were equal parts horror and joy. "You don't have to say a word. In fact, I think you can just call a guard over here and go back to your cell. I won't bother you again." I looked around me, at the crowded visiting room—families reuniting, lovers longing to touch, people coming to assuage a prisoner's loneliness out of the kindness of their hearts. No one like us... "Yeah, after murdering my Marc, maybe it's not too much to ask for a little help in understanding why."

He leaned a bit closer. His breath was rancid and his teeth were yellow, one of the front ones chipped. The beautiful promise of his youth had vanished, its only remaining signpost his piercing eyes, the color of sea glass.

"It was all your fault, you and that cunt mother of yours."

I'm nearly fifty years old, yet I can say with certainty this is the first time I'd ever heard anyone call my mother a cunt. If these words were spoken under different circumstances, I might have been shocked, appalled, might have stormed off.

But now I was simply disappointed that I didn't see it coming. "How so?" I wondered.

"Oh, don't play innocent with me. I know you two were always thick as thieves. You knew and she knew."

"What are you talking about?"

"When the pair of you sent me into the woods that night, on the Fourth."

I shrugged. "Best I can remember, I told you to go back there to take a piss."

"Yeah, yeah, it was all so innocent. Your mama really never told you? How she sold me up the river? Into bondage?" He shook his head, looked around the room. "Walker told me how she took money from him, a thousand bucks I think it was, if she'd lead him to me. And she did! How the hell else would he know exactly where to go? And which boy was prettier?" His smile was nightmarish and would haunt me, I knew, for a long time, probably the rest of my life.

I wouldn't need to ask Trudy to deny these accusations. I knew—in my bones, my heart, my gut, my head—that my mother would have never done such a thing. She'd told me herself how Walker had "found" Jeb—she'd invited the man to come with us and filled him in on all the details he'd need. It was all unwitting, in the hopes she could forge a relationship with a new man. But even without that information she naively gave, she wasn't the kind of soul who'd hand over an innocent boy to a predator to essentially be an abused and brainwashed slave to a very sick and dangerous man.

Trudy didn't have it in her. Not back then, not now, not ever. I knew this deep in my bones, my soul. There was no question.

But I wasn't about to argue. Jeb was convinced. There was certainty in his words—and undeniable resentment and hatred. He hated me; he hated Mom. Maybe blaming us was the only way he could reconcile what had happened to him and what he'd later done himself.

I nodded. "So, you found and killed my husband to get even?"

"That's right. Walker always told Hunter and me that if you wanna hurt a son-of-a-bitch, you don't hurt him, you hit where it'll really sting—hurt the person they love most. I thought about going after Trudy." He grinned again and I had a feeling I'd never be able to forget that twisted smile so far from anything joyous or friendly. "But Marc was *so* easy. So willing—a lamb to slaughter. Isn't that how the saying goes?" He smiled again. "God, he hated you!"

It wasn't true. Marc may have grown bored with me, tired of our life together, but I also knew, much the same as I knew the truth about my mother's culpability in all of this, that Marc never hated me.

"It was easy to seduce the little twerp," Jeb continued.

I'd had enough. Talk to an insane man and what are you going to get? Insanity. I scooted my chair back. This was a bad idea, and it definitely wasn't helping.

"What? You're gonna leave now? Didn't get the answers you hoped for? I ain't letting you off the hook so easy, faggot."

I stood.

All these years, I'd loved a phantom, a boy I wished for but who, in all likelihood, never existed. Perhaps I'd made the old Jeb up all those years ago, a heady brew of desire, Prince Charming, and balm for my questioning soul all at once.

I turned away, intending to head out the door, shaking and vulnerable, to head for the nearest bar. But there was something I was prepared to say to Jeb when I planned on coming here and, damn it, I would speak the words.

So, I turned back.

I met his gaze and ignored his smirk.

"You know I loved you once."

The enmity left his expression. His ashen skin color whitened even more. His mouth opened. I figured he might have been expecting rage and accusations, professions of hate. Those things he could deal with. But love? Obviously, that truly caught him off guard.

He looked as though he didn't know what to say. And that was okay, because I did.

"And believe it or not, I forgive you. Not because I can let go of what you did to me, but because of what forgiveness does for *me* now. It allows me to begin to heal from the wound you inflicted on my heart."

He was trying not to laugh. I didn't care. It was all an act, anyway. I'd reached him in a way he hadn't expected.

"Try to find the boy you were, if he ever was even real. I'd love to believe he's still in there somewhere. My Jeb."

I didn't wait for a response, but headed for the exit, clinging fast to the image of two boys swimming in the brownish-green currents of the Ohio River, one mistakenly believing he was the protector of the other.

But he halted my passage.

"Wait."

I sighed, now impatient to be free of him. I stood, waiting, without turning again to look at him.

"You asked me why. I never told you the real reason."

There was something in his voice—a kind of ache, of vulnerability—that now made me turn to look. He stared right at me as though he were trying to see inside. His eyes glistened.

"He chose me. No one ever did that before." He lowered his head. His shoulders shook once, twice. He raised his head, wiped his eyes with the back of his head. "Now go on, get the fuck out of here."

I kept my shoulders back, my head held high, and my tears at bay as I worked my way through the prison with its doors and guards.

He's human. He's damaged beyond repair. But he's human. And he once loved. He once hoped. But, save for me, had anyone ever loved him? Had those parents of his, so involved in their own addictions and pain, ever given him anything that resembled nurturing? Had he ever known the meaning of the word *family?*

Outside, I was relieved I wouldn't have to take the long and scary trip home via buses and trains. No, I had a ride.

Hunter waited for me outside.

I pictured him in the beat-up, fifteen-year-old Honda Civic he'd managed to acquire for his new job at Old Orchard Mall in Skokie, working as a sales assistant in the men's department at Nordstrom. He was doing great, surprising himself more than anyone else. His face was open, smiling, a welcome to a world I wasn't sure I still had access. His hair, now cut short, his green eyes, and the dark stubble that defined the contours of his jawline caused me to have an epiphany—this was the man I imagined Jeb would have, could have, grown up to be.

If only...

Outside, Hunter waited in the idling car, expectant and grateful for my approach. In the backseat, Vito popped up and gave out a single bark in greeting.

Hunter had come to me not to terrorize me, but to save me. And he would always be that—my savior and maybe, if things continued as they were, my love.

The End

Rick R. Reed is an award-winning and bestselling author of more than fifty works of published fiction. He is a Lambda Literary Award finalist. *Entertainment Weekly* has described his work as "heartrending and sensitive." *Lambda Literary* has called him: "A writer that doesn't disappoint..."

Rick lives in Palm Springs, CA, with his husband, Bruce, and their two rescue dogs, Kodi and Joaquin.

Excellent LGBTQ+ fiction by unique, wonderful authors.
Thrillers
Mystery
Romance
Young Adult
& More

Join our mailing list here for news, offers and free books!

Visit our website for more Spectrum Books
www.spectrum-books.com

Or find us on Instagram
@spectrumbookpublisher